MW00932048

BATTLE CRY

BASED ON A TRUE STORY

CASSLYNN POTTER

Copyright © 2021 Casslynn Potter, Casslynn McFadden
All rights reserved
First Edition

PAGE PUBLISHING, INC.
Conneaut Lake, PA

First originally published by Page Publishing 2021

ISBN 978-1-6624-3163-0 (pbk)
ISBN 978-1-6624-3164-7 (digital)

Printed in the United States of America

To Gabriella Younger, for supporting me through the most challenging times while in the process of writing this book. Veronica Ellis, Laura Shepley, and William Prevo, thank you for being able to create amazing drawings/graphics for my first book. Mr. David, for giving me the courage when others didn't. My Savior, thank you for everything you have done and will continue to do.

AUTHOR'S NOTE

As a survivor of sexual assault, I can't begin to tell you of how uncomfortable it was for me to sit down and take the time to write something that was so personal to me, yet something that was very much needed to be written and read about.

As I was growing up, a lot of people never knew what I was dealing with internally, especially my intermediate family and close friends. But, as the truth began to reveal itself, I found it hard to find those who I could relate to.

If anything, I felt like I was alone through it all.

Having the ability to write about such personal thoughts and some experiences that pertain to my life was hard…but *worth* it.

Although this book is realistic fiction, some of the incidents that do occur are relatable to my story, whereas some are not. To make this book more relatable to others who don't share the same experiences that I have, I began to implement more serial circumstances that do happen in people's everyday lives that most don't care to acknowledge or have the incapability to talk about due to the troubling distress the topic may bring.

Again, this is not *entirely* fiction.

I didn't want to write *Battle Cry* to not only share parts of my story but also to bring awareness to the various topics that some might not understand or talk about; this is so that they will have an understanding of what it is like for someone who has gone through severe trauma, by far that has the capability of wrecking one's mentality. Lastly, I wanted to write this book for those who are having a hard time with being able to cope with what has happened to them specifically—to let those who are still suffering know that you are *not* alone, and there *is* a light at the end of the tunnel.

I could lie and say that the pain that one's mentality has endured will remotely pass on as the time grows weary, but I wouldn't be honest with you. It is nothing but a process to fully come to terms with what has happened and who you are accepting to be. Only being eighteen, I have had the chance to be able to grow within these past seven years and, in the process, be able to forgive those who have done harm to me. Nonetheless, I have lived through it and have been able to move forward with my life without bearing nothing but happiness, and I hope that by reading this book, you will be able too.

Give and take, there will always be times where I can't help but dwell on what has happened, but rest assured, I know that I am not the only warrior out on the battlefield waiting for the chance for my cry to be heard.

Much love for you all,
Casslynn P.

Silence is the most powerful scream that no one can hear.

—Anonymous

PROLOGUE

"Cadence," he called.

As I was slowly beginning to get up from the couch, he shouted my name once more.

"Caa-denn-cce!" He shouted, only this time he was yelling my name out as if he had no idea of where I was.

As I approached the dull wooden bedroom door, I began to feel the goose bumps stand tall along my forearms.

Was I in trouble? Why was he calling for me so eagerly?

I placed my hand on the cold copper knob, and ever so slightly, I opened the door with apprehension. The room was dark as the night sky until I shut the door.

The night sky was now pitch black.

"Come here," he said.

I pictured the room's layout as I tried to direct myself from where my father's voice was coming from.

"Lie down."

I trembled in worry at the sound of his raspy voice. Once I stumbled upon his bed, I lie down next to him. When I finally made myself comfortable on the edge of the bed, my father moved in closer to me.

"Are you ready for your first lesson?" My father breathed in my ear.

The room became silent.

The room went still.

Even the air began to suffocate in silence, as I had.

I felt as if I was entrapped in a hollow tunnel, where both the exit and entrance had been closed off.

No way in, and no way out.

I didn't know what was worse at the time—the feeling that the situation was wrong or the feeling that I wasn't going to be rescued by anyone. *This was something that had not happened before, something that he had never done before.*

Seconds turned into minutes, and minutes became extensive moments, and before I knew it—he had told me to get out.

As I started to feel my crocodile tears roll down my rosy cheeks, I gathered my belongings.

I felt like I was missing something.

It had seemed like my strength of will had been stripped off my back and had been set by his side—where I was no longer in control of it.

I was at a loss for words.

Although I kept my head low, I walked out of the room in a hurry as my crocodile tears were now slipping away rapidly, just as a waterfall. Slowly and quietly, I wept on the brown worn down couch that had been isolated in the living room.

I felt as if I was in a daze of confusion of what had happened, and why he had caused me to feel like this?

The smell of tobacco that was embroidered on the brown worn down couch was more comforting to me than someone who I thought I could trust, someone who I thought wouldn't do anything to hurt me.

Why did he hurt me?

CHAPTER ONE
The Storm.

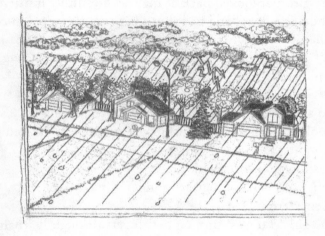

She was everything I wasn't.

Even on her imperfect days, she was still able to hold a graceful smile to anyone who had shared a glance with her. The way her long curly hair had cascaded past her shoulders had everyone glaring in envy.

Her effortless beauty had the ability to seize anyone's attention without even trying. The way that her eyes held a significant light-brown tint gave a unique reflection from the sunlight giving the most coruscating sight for sore eyes. Despite her features, she had a tall stature with a curvaceous frame that every girl would have ever dreamed of.

She was everything I wasn't.

"Cadence!"

I looked up and realized that she was staring at me with a blank expression written across her face.

"Did you even hear what I said?"

I shook my head side to side, flustered with embarrassment.

"It's okay. It wasn't even important anyways." She laughed it off.

She looked back up at the mirror that hung high in the girl's bathroom and started to comb through her long curly hair with her fingers. I stared at her then looked to the second mirror that hung lower than hers.

The girl that looked back at me was dreadfully horrifying. She was as short as a dwarf and had short, frizzy, curly hair. Although she was similar in the figure to the girl next to her, she could easily point out every flaw that her body had. The girl that was staring back at me was hideous.

I was hideous.

"So are we still hanging out tonight after school?"

I looked away from the girl in the mirror and noticed that she was talking to me.

"Yeah, of course," I said.

"I'm so excited! We haven't hung out in a while."

"Genevieve."

The girl who was running her fingers through her hair turned to me and smiled.

"Yes, Cadence?"

I froze in silence, trying to think about how I should approach my insecurities as a topic to discuss. My mind was racing. This girl was my best friend, and somehow I couldn't even stand the thought of telling her how I truly feel or even discussing what went unsaid for what felt like a lifetime.

"Uhm…just send a text when you are able to stop by," I said.

Genevieve gave me a half smile.

"Are you okay?"

I looked down at the bathroom ground and noticed every crack that the tiles had possessed, giving off the imperfect details that had made the bathroom flawed. The cement that had sealed the tiles together was slowly beginning to crumble underneath the treacherous feet of those who paraded through the bathrooms without even using the utilities—just to skip class. Without even looking up, I could only say the one thing that could come to my mind.

"Yeah, why wouldn't I be?" I said, grinning a smile that one could only try so hard to fake.

It was the sixth hour, the last hour of the school day until the weekend could finally begin. All I wanted to do was sit back in my assigned seat without having to come to terms with doing any homework that I knew would be due on Monday until Sunday night.

Procrastinating? I sure am.

For my sixth hour, I had psychology with Mr. Murray.

Mr. Murray was my favorite teacher. He was as tall as Jack's beanstalk, attained ocean blue eyes, had brown hair that was slowly beginning to fade into gray, and always greeted his students with his flashing broad smile. Overall, for only being in his late fifties, he did not look a day over forty-five.

Mr. Murray always strived to educate his students on the science that tries to understand the way people think, feel, and act in different ways, but he also tried to incorporate moral principles in his lesson plans, to try to do more than educate his students on his expected teaching curriculum.

As the minute bell was down to its last remaining seconds, I rushed to take my seat. I always personally asked the teachers to be seated by the nearest window, only if it was present. Mr. Murray's classroom was one of the biggest classrooms that Arkseley High School had to offer, with an amazing view that had peered through the looking glass.

Arkseley had always fancied our football team, regardless if we won or lost against our rivalries, so it doesn't come as a surprise of how incredibly new the bleachers were or even the freshly planted grass that was covered with the same markings but reeked of the brand-new paint. Behind the football field were two ginormous hills that sprouted different colored wildflowers that had laid on top of one another. In between the hills, the sun had always had a cozy place to rest. The sky above had never neglected to reflect the sunlight that had come to be visible, giving off the most brilliant blue. The clouds were always to be seen in endless shapes as they slowly drifted in and out of sight. The view from the window had stricken every one of Mr. Murray's students' interests, and luckily, I was the one able to be seated next to its perpetuating beauty.

I sat down in my seat next to the window on the far right of the room. The majority of the class was either on their phones, talking to one another or walking in tardy by the time the last minute bell went off.

The class had started to gather its attention at the sight of Mr. Murray writing on his chalkboard. In his perfect cursive, he wrote, "What is the meaning of being found? And how do we determine if we are found?" Mr. Murray had set the white chalk along the side of the chalkboard and stepped back. As he was still facing the chalkboard, he looked at it as if he was looking for the missing piece of the puzzle. As if puzzled in confusion, he walked to his desk placed in the center view of the board and sat down in his sturdy leather chair. With his piercing blue eyes, he stared at everyone as if he was watching us closely. As his gaze slowly divagated from one student to another, he locked eyes with an underclassman who sat to the left of me. The student had always equipped herself in fancy jewelry as if showing off her luxuries to enhance the belief that she was better than any of the other students.

"Remi, would you care to elaborate on what's on the board?" Mr. Murray said, resting his hands on the top of his head.

The underclassman looked at Mr. Murray with a clueless facial expression.

"Uhhhh, I don't know what to exactly *elaborate* on." She said as she sat there fixated on the prompt like it was rocket science.

As Remi slouched back in her seat, Mr. Murray began to skim the room once again.

"Any volunteers?" he asked.

I looked around the room.

Every student was trying their best to either avoid any eye contact with Mr. Murray or just stare at the chalkboard, trying their best to come up with a reasonable answer.

While the room began to fall into quietude, I couldn't help but direct my attention toward the perpetuating beauty that was to the right of me.

The sun was no longer in the midst between the two hills, as the sky was now turning into a dark gray, and the clouds had gathered together in an army.

It was the beginning of a storm.

"You shouldn't be so close to the window, Cadence," he said.

My father was sitting on the brown worn down couch that he had admired so much. Sitting back while drinking a glass of whiskey, my father was carefully observing me.

The sky cried white, hard clumps of hail and was making loud boom sounds. Only being eight years old, I would never fail to feel empathy for the sky.

Was the sky unhappy?

Could it not help but express its pain through its sad wails for help?

"Dammit, Cadence!"

At the sound of his horrid yell, I turned my head to capture the whiskey glass to my forehead.

The pain that emerged from the glass was so substantial—not only did the pain take over my forehead, but was also slowly beginning to travel to my left eye. As I could feel the sting the pain was enacting, I could feel nothing more than guilt to have moved away from the window.

I didn't listen, and this was my punishment.

"Now look what you've made me do! Are you incapable of listening to me? How am I supposed to clean you up before she comes here tomorrow to pick you up!" His voice echoed through the entire house as the storm was wailing even louder. As the glass shards steadily started to burrow underneath my skin, my eyes developed the tears that staggered downward my face. In fear, I picked myself up and ran to the bathroom.

I couldn't help but realize that the storm wasn't only crying out for itself, but for me as well.

Ever since that night, I couldn't help but continuously recall the *bangs* and *booms* that followed each thunder, getting more anxious after another.

I hated storms.

"Cadence, maybe you would be willing to tell me what the prompt is implying?"

Astonished that he chose me, I only had a few moments to gather my thoughts to think of something that would make some sense.

My eyes averted to Mr. Murray and then back to the chalkboard, "What is the meaning of being found? And how do we determine if we are found?"

"Uhm, I think the prompt is saying that in order to be *found*, we need to be *lost*. When we are lost, we have the tendency to think that we always need some sort of redemption. Even when we are lost, we always seek out someone or something to have the capability to take us out of what made us believe that we are lost—whether the belief may derive from depression, skepticism, heartache, or the feeling of being weak. But when we are found, we are able to feel the relief of being saved from what has made us lost. Being found, we are no longer enclosed in isolation. We aren't abandoned in our empty thoughts or even left to believe that we are alone. We are found." I said.

Mr. Murray looked at me and gave me his broad, flashing smile—carried away with amusement.

Throughout the bus ride home, I was anxious.

The wind was howling against everything that was in its way—mailboxes, signposts, traffic lights, even the branches that hung on every tree. The storm continued to cry, not having a care if anyone despised its wails for help. Although Genevieve had texted me earlier of the time she was going to come over, I still didn't know if I could even begin to explain a slither of how I truly felt about everything—what *happened* to me for so long that even she didn't know of.

The walk home from the bus stop was shorter than it usually was, given the fact that I couldn't stand being wet and was running like a wild dog all the way home.

"Cadence! I want you to meet someone."

Just as I walked through the door, I noticed my mom was sitting next to a complete stranger on our couch.

My mom was stunningly perfect. She had long curly blonde hair with dark-blue eyes and amazingly straight teeth. She worked at one of our local hospitals nearby as a registered nurse on the NTICU floor. Given she was at the top of her class, she was a highly respected nurse on her unit—everyone knew if they had a problem or needed critical advice pertaining to their work, they all could go to her.

"Hello, nice to meet you. I'm Lee."

The random stranger was sitting next to my mom with his hand resting on her lap—smiling slyly as if he had received a cookie from answering a question correctly. Regardless of being African American, he had thin gray glasses that were too small for his enormous head and a stiff gigantic belly that stood out enough for him to rest his hands on.

Why was this *Lee* guy so comfortable with my mom when I haven't even heard anything about him?

"Uhm…hi," I said while taking off my overly run-down Converse and placing them by the front door.

Awkward as I felt, I knew that whatever was going on wasn't going to last. My mom had never believed in labels, but neither did she ever liked the idea of being *single*.

She had always known how to attract the wrong guys despite her beauty, but above all, her intellect.

"Wow, did someone not have a good day at school?" My mom said.

"Helen, it's okay. She's not going to get to know me right off the bat. It takes time," Lee said.

I couldn't help but roll my eyes at the sound of his optimistic tone of voice. Lee really thinks that this thing of a "relationship" will last? He really believes that I would *want* to get to know him?

How self-assuring.

"Well, Genevieve is planning on coming over in twenty minutes," I said.

My mom gave me a shake of her hand, meaning "go away," and then proceeded to chat with Lee—giggling and flipping her hair as if she were a schoolgirl.

I walked to my room and sat on my bed.

The walls were covered in a light gray with my white door and white trim, framing each border and corner. The window by my bed was huge that held an arch shape. Behind the glass was an oak tree that stood strong with its branches flailing against one another as the wind caressed its leaves.

Moments passed by before I heard two knocks on my door. As the door slowly crept open, a girl stood in the doorframe drenched from her hair, all the way down to her shoes in the storm's cries.

"Hey, Cadence!" She said, smiling so wide that she didn't feel like she was bothered from being wet.

"Hey, Genevieve," I said.

It still amazed me how, even on a rainy day, Genevieve was still able to hold a smile. How could such a positive person be best friends with someone like myself?

Genevieve walked into my room and closed the door behind her.

"So tell me, what's wrong? Lately, you've been acting deranged. And I mean this in the best way possible, but you're really starting to worry me," Genevieve said.

My gaze went from her to look upon the big oak tree that stood magnificently tall, with only centimeters away from the window. My breathing steadily increased, giving off a fog on the cold surface of the window.

"I have been trying to put it off for the longest time," I said, trying to manage the race my heart was beating to.

"I just want you to know that I love you and that I'll always be here for you *no matter what*. Whatever you are dealing with is no match for not only you but also for me. You are my best friend. You always have and never will stop being my best friend," she said.

I looked down at the palm of my hands and noticed that the teardrops that had fallen were being caught.

Genevieve and I grew up on the same street ever since pre-school, and throughout the time that had passed, I still hadn't told her of what happened to me. We are seniors now, and I still didn't tell her what has been affecting me from such a young age.

"No one would understand or even care to believe me...including you," I said.

I looked at her, knowing well enough that everything I was internally dealing with would be too much to ask of her to listen to. I grew up with the trauma and being told that "*no one would listen to you. No one would believe you. You're just a number among countless who don't even care about you.*"

"Try me." She said.

As hesitation mustered within me, I felt like I *needed* to tell someone, but how could I?

I locked eye contact with her. She knew me like no one could as I knew everything that was to know about her. She knew everything about me, except the hidden secret I kept hidden from her. What best friend would I be if I didn't tell her?

Then I knew it was time to tell someone, my best friend.

CHAPTER TWO
Ain't All Moonshine and Rainbows.

Although I was Caucasian and African American, the majority of the people in my suburb looked at me as if I was out of sorts—just because I had maintained a mocha complexion and had coiled hair. No one really cared if my mom was white. All they had concerned themselves with was the idea that my brother and I were not fully white, and we didn't look like them. My brother Lance was nothing but protective of me.

Whenever we decided to go outside and play basketball or even catch some sunlight, he would always have to shield me or make me look the other way if he caught the neighbors giving us a disgusted glance.

He never cared about what our neighbors thought of us.

With being one shade darker than me, black curly hair, deep-brown intimidating eyes, and a personality that would have anyone cracking up, he was always a sight for sore eyes. Never had he asked the attention that others would give him, whether it would be good or bad—but mostly good. Whenever someone had invited him to a birthday party or even something after school, he would always say, *"Well, I guess Cadence will be excited to come along!"* He never left me out of anything that could occupy his time—not because he felt the *need* to, but because he *wanted* to. Despite being a year older than me, he never made me feel like there was rivalry pitted within our relationship. Instead, Lance showed so much compassion for our bond to become stronger. Even with him being a year older than I, he never gave in to the superiority that he could've conveyed as easily as another pair of siblings.

I really missed Lance.

Ever since he had moved to live on campus at Central Michigan University, he felt that it was fit to always write letters to me, that I could collect and keep them as reminders that he still cared for me, even while being miles away. In correspondence with every letter that was mailed to me from him, I always wrote back. Whenever I wrote back, I couldn't disregard his occasional letters that would read, *"I miss you,"* and *"How have things been at home?"* With being miles away, Lance still never gave up on what he had left behind.

Not only was Lance my protector against those who lived nearby us, but also as the person who protected me from whom I lived with.

My mother, Helen, was an unusual character.

Even though she was amazing at what she worked as, she had always spent her free time involving herself with the most trouble-some men and going to the bar—knowing that she could easily rely on those around her to pay for her drinks.

"Cadence!"

The sound of my name rang through my ears as the harsh vibrations from someone yelling set course to my eardrums, soon to burst from such a horrific outcry.

With as much energy I could possibly have, I sat up straight in my bed.

"What the—" I said.

My eyes flickered endlessly as my sight was slowly trying to piece together my distorted vision.

"You, little girl…get up!" A woman shouted.

As my vision became clear, so did the situation that was before me.

My white wooden bedroom door was opened wide to notice that my mom was standing between two men of whom I didn't even know. My mom could be seen wearing a tight-fitting shirt that had exposed her cleavage and wore blue jeans that had been worn out past its usage. With her blonde curly hair tangled in a crazed mess, I could see her eyes faintly as they were bloodshot with a hint of crimson.

The man to the left of her had looked as if he had run a marathon, for his clothes looked soaked and was barely grasping onto his body.

The man to the right of her was looking around my room until he looked back at me with a dreadful, snooty glare.

"Who is she?" The man to the right of Helen said, raising an eyebrow in interest.

Helen pulled out a steel flask that was tucked behind her and put it to her lips. With dissatisfaction, she gave the flask a few shakes and flipped it upside down in the air.

"Aww, no more!" Helen said.

The man to the left of her took the flask and examined it. Both had given the empty vacant a pout and then started laughing uncontrollably.

As Helen and the man to her left were occupied in their own hysteria, the man on the right began to stride in my direction.

When the man of the right stooped to my level on the bed, the exotic scent of vodka escaped his breath—burning my keen sense of smell.

"You look like a pretty little girl. How old are you?" The man said.

"Nine," I replied, as my voice started to shake in fear.

With every exhale the man breathed, another goose bump would arise on my arms.

"Such a pretty girl for only being nine," the man said with a weary smirk as he started to caress the side of my right cheek.

As uncomfortable as I felt, Helen stared at me from across the room. Aware of the situation, she was still perched by the door, along with the man from her left. She was watching me as an owl would watch the night.

The night could easily fall into catastrophe, and she would still be resting upon a branch as the crisis before her grew hectic. Helen Palmer was an owl, an owl who stood still and became a bystander to the night's calamity.

The strange man, who was far too intimate with me, waved over the man from Helen's left.

As the man of the left approached my bedside, the creepy man who was invading my personal space gestured to the man of the left to look at me closely. As the man on the right got off the bed to stand near me, the other guy had taken his place next to me.

The man of the left looked much younger than the man of the right. The man of the left had emerald eyes that held a spark of sanity left to spare and blonde hair that shagged just above his almond-shaped eyes. Those emerald gems followed the trail of the outline of my body then back up to my face.

I couldn't help but fail to recognize the familiarity that both of the men shared. The uncomfortable tension that had resided within me was far too recognizable, as the feeling never failed to give my demeanor warnings ahead of what was to happen.

"Don't you believe she is as pretty as I said she was?" The man of the right said to the man of the left.

The man of the left smiled and nodded his head.

As the man of the left proceeded to gain more proximity of my personal space, the man of the right began to make his way on my bed— inching his way closer to me.

As the predators were aware of their prey, I couldn't help but direct my attention to Helen.

Entirely aware of what was happening, Helen still remained leaning against the doorframe, fiddling with her empty flask. Her amusement was nonetheless noticeable of a child and carried no shame nor guilt upon her youthful middle-age expression.

Out of all the love for a daughter, this was the most discerning her love could've ever shown. Even though she obtained alcohol in her system, she didn't give a care in the world of what was happening right before her.

She just stood there.

The man of the right ran his fingers through his jet-black hair and furrowed his eyebrows—causing his forehead to wrinkle as a raisin is to prune.

"Go with Helen. I can take it from here!" The man of the right yelled as he nudged the man of the left in the direction off the bed.

The man of the left got up and directed his eyes to Helen. She was still leaning up against the doorframe, but she shook her head strenuously from side to side. Helen's pupils were bigger than the moon itself, as they were radiating denial for even being looked at by the man of the left.

"She doesn't look like she wants to do anything, Dad," the son said to the dad as he made his way back onto the bed.

Is this what father and son usually do?

They act as if they are a venus flytrap. The vulnerable prey sits upon the leaves, the predator is able to imprison the poor victim. Why must the food chain declare these informal sacrifices? If the food chain proclaims its need for such sacrifice, then it must be that way.

My hope for escape was no more.

The father grunted slowly as he began to fiddle with the strings that were attached to my care bear pajama pants.

Through my silent tears, I couldn't help but hear a slight amount of laughter coming from the other side of the room.

Although I wasn't deserted physically, I was deserted mentally.

My mom was supposed to be my anchor that could hold me down in the moments when I needed to stay afloat. Yet, all she did was break off her attachment to the one thing that needed her the most. When did she break off?

Since when did she sever ties with me?

As I saw the care bears begin to fall steadily toward a lower position, I braced myself for the worst that was to come...

While my eyes were closed tightly, I heard a few shuffles of the feet, and that's when I opened my eyes to see Lance standing above the father, son, and I.

"What the hell is going on? You're not going to do anything about this? Get the hell off her right now!" Lance said, gesturing to Helen as if she had lost her mind.

Taking a grip onto the father's blue flannel shirt, Lance swung him far away from me, slamming his back against the wall. Lance then aggressively pushed the son back, causing the son to fall backward off the bed.

With the tears that were no longer filling the streams running down my face, I sat up in my bed. Thankful for his rescue, I embraced Lance's hug he offered. Sitting down next to me, Lance gave a shooting glare at Helen.

"You are a piece of work..." Lance uttered.

Long since, I wasn't able to peacefully fall asleep without waking up in the dead of night—in hopes no one would barge in, nor care to. Neither have my mom and I talked about what happened when I was nine, partially because she doesn't remember.

But I do.

CHAPTER THREE
The Lessons.

"Cadence, would you pass me the sugar?"

As I was about to pass the sugar to little ten-year-old Genevieve, I remembered how she forgot one little detail of having teatime.

"I think someone forgot to use their manners," I said sternly.

"Please pass me the sugar?" Little Genevieve slightly tilted her head and gave an adorable flash of a smile.

I gave her a smile back and proceeded to laugh amongst our little playdate.

Genevieve was the only friend that I had growing up. Whenever I wanted to play a certain game or even play a game of pretend, she didn't fuss against it. Overall, she was just as happy as to do anything with me. Regardless of what we were doing, she and I always looked forward to being able to spend time with one another.

Genevieve was sipping her cup of tea that contained no substance inside, continuing to believe that she was, in fact, sipping actual tea.

As I sat my empty cup down on the plastic chipped saucer plate, I began to observe the table where Genevieve and I had our teatime.

It was a purple plastic table with pink silverware, along with pink kiddy cups and saucer plates. Although everything was heavily used, we were always content with what we had to play with.

As I brought my attention back to Genevieve, I could see that she was holding her pinky up as she still had the pink teacup to her pursed lips.

"Cadence, I'm off. Don't forget that your dad is coming to pick you up in about ten minutes!" Helen said as she was rushing to the door with stilettos as high as Rapunzel's tower.

With a slam of the door, she was gone.

"Is she going to work in those heels?" Genevieve questioned.

"No, she's going to meet a friend," Lance said as he had plopped on the floor next to our plastic table, knowing all too well of the familiarity of what Helen was really leaving for.

There were so many reasons as to why I would think Helen would leave whenever she didn't have to work.

Did she not love Lance and I?

Did we do something wrong?

Did I do something wrong?

My thoughts were suddenly deviating from one generalization to the next, thinking of why Helen miraculously disappears whenever I think I need her the most.

In the stillness of the room, I felt a warm comfort on my shoulder.

"Hey, are you okay?" Genevieve questioned.

I looked at her with an assuring smile. "Yeah. Why wouldn't I be?" I said.

With disbelief, Genevieve sat back and turned her head to Lance.

As if Genevieve was dropping a hint, Lance looked to me and spoke. "Cad, are you sure you're okay?"

What could I say?

The unusual normality of me telling them that I felt abandoned every time Helen walked out that door, how I felt as if I was entrapped in a box that was left on the side of the street, left there to be unheard and unseen.

To be able to tell them even though I had their comfort, it wasn't good enough?

How could I easily tell them such?

So I nodded my head and faked a smile.

Genevieve and Lance were no fools. As much as I had pretended to carry on the facade of being okay, they knew all too well of my white lies.

"I didn't know that your dad was coming to get you today," Genevieve said.

I couldn't help but feel disheartened at the thought of not wanting to go with my father for the weekend. Knowing that my father was a good man at heart, he could sometimes be a little harsh when it came to certain things.

If anything, the man was unpredictable.

"I just remembered when she said something about it before she left," I said as I referred to Helen mentioning how I'm going to my father's house for the weekend.

Genevieve smiled at me and then gave a sigh, loud enough that it would make just about everyone turn their heads and look at her as if she was searching for any attention.

"Well, I guess that means I have to go home." Genevieve pouted.

She put her teacup on the saucer plate and pushed back her chair.

"Hey, if you need a ride, my dad and I can take you home. You live just right up the street," I pointed out.

Genevieve lived in an adorable small house with a pastel yellow door with the exterior being a light gray and shutters being a dark gray that had sat on the sides of the two ginormous windows. In comparison to my house, hers was more thrilling to the eye than mine that had a boring beige color and red shutters that had not complemented anything in their entire existence.

"Are you sure?" Genevieve questioned.

Before I could nod my head, there was a sudden ring of the doorbell.

Lance jumped to his feet and made his way to the front door.

With one open swing, the door swung to reveal my father.

"Hey, Lance," my father said, as he stood as stiff as a pencil.

Once they had greeted one another, my father made his strides toward me.

"Are you ready to go, Cadence?" My father said.

"Yes, but do you think we can drop off Genevieve? She lives right up the street...please?"

My father looked from me to Genevieve and slouched his shoulders.

"I guess. But we have to hurry 'cause I have something planned for us," he sternly spoke.

As I began to gather my change of clothes for the weekend, Genevieve and I then made our way toward the front door.

Lance was hovering by the entrance silently, as he was waiting patiently for all three of us to walk out the door he was politely holding open.

"Goodbye, Cadence." Lance smiled as he wrapped his arms around me.

"Bye, Lance," I said.

Despite the fact that Lance and I didn't share the same father, his father had not wanted anything to do with him, and for that, I yearned to bring him with us. Even though it would be a good idea to mention him tagging along, my father wouldn't allow it since he would have to contact my mom about bringing Lance—which he even hates doing now to make plans with me.

As Genevieve said her goodbyes to Lance, she and I both hopped into my father's dirt brown 2000 Chevrolet Silverado.

In a matter of a few minutes, we had reached Genevieve's house.

"Thank you, Leavan, for taking me home," Genevieve said as she got out of the truck. "And thank you, Cadence, for having me for tea!" She smiled and then shut the door to the truck.

With each step that Genevieve took, she bounced with excitement.

"That's a nice friend you got there. She has polite manners," my father said.

I didn't say anything, but alone in my thoughts, I couldn't agree more.

As we backed out of Genevieve's driveway, we headed toward my second home.

As the distance to get to my father's house felt like an eon, I watched the outside world that was flowing fast past us.

"Cadence..."

I looked from the window to see my father concentrated on his peripheral view.

"Yes?"

"I understand that you're growing up and how only being ten years old can be a little scary. I mean, double digits can be a little scary without the proper guidance," he stated.

At first, I wasn't quite sure about what he was talking about. Even so, I was confused as to why he would bring up my age when we celebrated it a couple of months ago.

"Since you are of age now, I am going to have to teach and show you things that a ten-year-old needs to know so they won't be scared when the time comes for you to really grow up."

The house was smaller than my mom's, but with my father living alone, he had nothing to complain about. He personally loved how his property was low maintenance, and the neighborhood was friendly.

"All right, listen up, Cadence," my father said, as he sat me down beside him on the brown couch he adorn so much.

As he placed my hands in his, he started to speak again.

"Now there are going to have to be some ground rules before I can start teaching you."

I nodded my head. Everything that my father was saying to me was confusing. I thought that school had been the only environment for teaching kids of my age.

"The first rule is that you need to obey me. Obedience is key if you want to learn something from what I am teaching you. If you refuse to do as I ask, then there will be severe consequences. We don't want that, do we?"

"No," I stated.

"That's my little girl." He smiled and caressed the palm of his hand against my cheek.

"The second rule is after we're done with our lessons, you need to wash up. It's important that you remember to take a bath when we are done because then you will be ready and set for our next lesson. Personal

hygiene is one of the most major adolescent roles in our lessons. If you do not keep up with your hygiene, then there will be severe consequences."

I nodded my head.

"The last, but most important rule of them all, is to never tell anyone of what I am teaching you. But like I said, what I am teaching you will help you be able to not be scared when the actual opportunity presents itself to you. If you do tell anyone, then I am forced to have to do something that we both might regret." My father's smile turned into a frown, pretending as if he was pouting, then started to clench my hands tightly.

"Just think of the lessons as playing pretend. You'll enjoy it," my father said, as he let go of my poor-aching hands.

As I brought my hands closer to me, I noticed that my hands were beginning to turn a harsh red from the pressure that my father had implemented onto them.

Whether or not I wanted to oblige with my father's lessons, there was no doubt that his strength was nevertheless wary of being feeble.

"Do you understand the rules, Cadence?" My father asked.

I picked up my head and foreseen something that I thought wasn't possible.

Someone who I thought was a good man at heart with his quirks, was now someone who had possessed nothing but his quirks. My father had turned from a modest man to an undoubtedly boastful person who could be seen through as someone who desired something that he wanted, but couldn't tame.

He had become someone quite unfamiliar.

"Answer me, Cadence." My father's tone was to be heard throughout the entire house.

In fright of his sudden response, I answered back with a "yes."

"Good! Now that everything has been addressed, we are going to begin with the first lesson today."

My father got up and proceeded to walk toward his bedroom. Halfway to his bedroom, my father came to a halt and turned to look at me.

"When I call you, come. Then we will begin our lesson."

As time moved slowly, I sat on the couch and waited until the time came for him to call my name.

"Cadence," he called.

As I was slowly beginning to get up from the couch, he shouted my name once more.

"Caa-denn-cce!" He shouted, only this time he was yelling my name out as if he had no idea of where I was.

As I approached the dull wooden bedroom door, I began to feel the goose bumps stand tall along my forearms.

Was I in trouble? Why was he calling for me so eagerly?

I placed my hand on the cold copper knob, and ever so slightly, I opened the door with apprehension. The room was dark as the night sky until I shut the door.

The night sky was now pitch black.

"Come here," he said.

I pictured the room's layout as I tried to direct myself from where my father's voice was coming from.

"Lie down."

I trembled in worry at the sound of his raspy voice. Once I stumbled upon his bed, I lie down next to him.

When I finally made myself comfortable on the edge of the bed, my father moved closer to me.

"Are you ready for your first lesson?" My father breathed in my ear.

The room became silent.

The room went still.

Even the air began to suffocate in silence, as I had.

I felt as if I was entrapped in a hollow tunnel, where both the exit and entrance had been closed off.

No way in, and no way out.

I didn't know what was worse at the time—the feeling that the situation was wrong or the feeling that I wasn't going to be rescued by anyone. This was something that had not happened before, something that he had never done before.

Seconds turned into minutes, and minutes became extensive moments, and before I knew it—he had told me to get out.

As I started to feel my crocodile tears roll down my rosy cheeks, I gathered my belongings.

I felt like I was missing something.

It had seemed like my strength of will had been stripped off my back and had been set by his side—where I was no longer in control of it.

I was at a loss for words.

Although I kept my head low, I walked out of the room in a hurry as my crocodile tears were now slipping away rapidly, just as a waterfall. Slowly and quietly, I wept on the brown worn down couch that had been isolated in the living room.

I felt as if I was in a daze of confusion of what had happened, and why he had caused me to feel like this?

The smell of tobacco that was embroidered on the brown worn down couch was more comforting to me than someone who I thought I could trust, someone who I thought wouldn't do anything to hurt me.

Why did he hurt me?

CHAPTER FOUR
Nothing More, Nothing Less.

I was always consumed in my own thoughts.

I had the ability to shield my true self by hiding behind some persona that I couldn't even take credit for. I had mastered the art of keeping my feelings at bay and to the point where no one would become suspicious of any personal conflicting problems. I had made a fool out of everyone for not recognizing.

Let alone would I believe it was I who was really making a fool out of myself. I thought that I could hide behind a mask without revealing anything, but what I didn't know is that the mask could only sustain so much until it had reached its breaking point, and my mask was bursting at its seams.

So I took off that mask when I told Genevieve.

I opened myself up to someone whom I should've told from the start but was too afraid.

I became vulnerable.

I poured my feelings into her glass in hopes that she would drink, and she did.

Not only was I surprised that she was able to believe me, but she also *listened* to me.

"Oh, Cadence…" Genevieve said with sympathy as she wrapped her arms around me, giving off a warm embrace.

For the rest of the night, Genevieve and I continued to converse about what had happened—what I had not only told her but many for so long. By the end of the night, Genevieve was home as I lay in my bed wide-awake.

I felt relieved by the time Genevieve went home. The untold truth that I had kept buried underneath my mask was screaming out for someone to pay attention, to *listen* to me.

Who would've known that the most unspoken person has the most powerful scream for help that no one can hear?

It's already been a week since I told Genevieve, and I still felt that I am carrying around the baggage that has only become lighter by a feather. Not only have I been depressed, but I have also been in distress.

It was my senior year, and it felt as though it was just yesterday that the school year had begun. Now it is the beginning of a new year and a new semester.

To say the least, I was behind on everything that needed to be done for me to graduate high school. I haven't ordered my cap and gown, nor have I had any intention of making future plans. It felt as though I am running a mile in the same direction but not getting anywhere.

I was stranded.

As I was leaning against my locker, I watched every student pass by me. It was crazy to believe that I was going to be graduating in four months. With everything I was going through as of now, I'm not ready.

How could I be ready?

When someone graduates high school, they move on in their life. They find better things to do. They focus on their goals and their life's meaning—accomplish them and eventually become happier as life gets better for them. But how could I be ready for that?

How could I even get to where I want to be if I am stuck in the same place as I have been for years, yet I try to move, and I get nowhere?

A feeling that easily swallows me whole, just as fast as quicksand.

The constant feeling that I will never amount to anything as long as I stay where I cannot prosper, where I am persistently battling with myself.

The feeling of just being less valuable than a penny and having no hopes for what the bringing is to come. The wandering thoughts of believing that I will not have a future, just because my past is still chained to me—the chains that hope to drag me down in the rekus of no future, no hope.

Yet, I still stand and drag the chains that slow me down in a constant circumference of defeat.

My life has been nothing of misery, but how could I hope for something that seems so far out of my reach?

As I pushed myself off my locker, I proceeded to Mr. Murray's class that had waited for me.

When I walked into the classroom, I had seen no student in my sight but Mr. Murray at his desk, grading papers with his red pen.

"I apologize for being a little tardy, but where is the class?"

"You're standing in it," Mr. Murray expressed with humor.

"Oh, no… I meant the students?" I stated.

Mr. Murray had set his stack of papers aside and motioned for me to sit down at one of the isolated chairs in front of his desk.

"So where are the students?" I said as discomfort was slowly starting to stir within me.

No matter what role the person had in my life, I had always got uncomfortable around any guy. I was too afraid that something could happen that I wouldn't even allow myself to be alone with a guy.

I couldn't stand the thoughts that were always at the back of my mind.

"Today is one of the assemblies for the snowcoming week. Every student was to report to the gymnasium right after lunch. Why aren't you there?" Mr. Murray said.

Snowcoming was something that Arskeley had done after homecoming. Basically, snowcoming consisted of a week of school spirit but has a dance called *Sadies*, where the girls have to ask the guys out for a chance. Practically, I just think of it as being a week where all you see are high school sweethearts jamming their tongues down their significant other's throats. PDA was something that no one could control.

Everyone in high school has raging hormones.

"Oh, I forgot about the assembly," I said absentmindedly.

With everything that has been currently occupying my mind, I didn't really give a thought about certain events that were taking place.

"Well, since I have the time to talk, how are you doing?" Mr. Murray asked as he sat back in his leather chair.

"I've never been better than ever," I smiled slyly, hoping that he could take the bait I was dangling in front of his eyes. "I should probably head to the assembly now." I got up and started pacing my way out of the classroom.

"Wait, right there."

As socially awkward as I felt, he was still someone of high authority.

How could I not listen to *my teacher*?

It would feel wrong if I didn't.

I stopped in my tracks and turned to look at Mr. Murray, still sitting in his leather chair.

"Come back. I wasn't finished talking to you yet," He abruptly said.

I walked back to the isolated chair placed in front of his desk and plopped down.

"Now are you really going to tell me what's going on, or do I need to fail you on your assignment?" He said.

"What assignment?"

"The one where you tell me how personal problems affect students' lives to the point where it psychologically distracts them in my class?" Mr. Murray folded his arms over one another as he raised his eyebrow.

How come the only teacher I could stand is cornering me like this? I didn't know that this was an intervention.

"Shouldn't you be at the assembly like the other teachers?" I folded my arms over one another in mockery.

"I'm not the other teachers, I'm just concerned, and all I want to know is if you're fine. A simple yes or no will suffice." Mr. Murray said.

I unfolded my arms.

No one had really cared to ask me how I was doing.

Although it had bothered me that no one asked, here I was being defiant with someone who does care to ask me.

"No."

"What's wrong?" Mr. Murray asked as he showed concern by leaning against his desk, as I had grabbed his undivided attention.

"Anything I tell you is student and teacher confidentiality, right?" I hesitated.

Mr. Murray nodded his head and then let out a sigh. "As long as you are safe and not thinking of any life-threatening thoughts, then yes."

As much as it occurred to me of my depression, suicide had been on the back burner.

I never really wanted to give it any thought because I wanted to have the opportunity of trying to fix what was wrong with me.

"It's just that I have gone through a lot growing up, and it hasn't really been an issue for me to go on with my day until recently. So much had happened that I can't process the thought of trying to get over it, but I want to move on with my life. It's my senior year, and I am still having a hard time dealing with everything. I just want to finally be able to breathe in the air that I never got a chance to breathe in, to be free of these horrendous burdens that I continue to live with. But I can't. The past is wearing me down, and all I can look forward to after high school is knowing that I was able to graduate. Nothing more, nothing less."

"If I may ask, what happened in the past that is bothering you right now?" He asked intriguingly.

"Why do you want to know? I don't see you asking every other one of your students the same question," I said.

Mr. Murray was taken aback by my off comment but suddenly had relaxed his intense posture and expression.

"Because you're a bright student, Cadence. One of the few who I know is more than capable of succeeding. But you cannot succeed if there is something that is holding you back from it. Don't think that I haven't noticed a drastic change in your behavior from the beginning of the school year. I know that you are feeling alone, maybe even vulnerable. This is only because you feel as though you are fighting something that is troubling you alone," Mr. Murray sympathetically spoke.

"I'm sorry. I just never thought that you would care to know."

"No need to apologize. If you don't want to talk to me about what happened, that's totally up to you. I don't want to force you into opening up if you don't want to allow yourself to."

Mr. Murray was one of Arkseley's well-respected teachers and who anyone didn't have a problem with. He was literally someone who anyone could talk to about anything without feeling like you were forced to do or say anything.

He was a listener rather than a talker.

The only one who I opened myself up to was Genevieve, and I didn't think that I would be able to tell anyone else. Despite not telling Genevieve, I had felt for the longest time that no one cared for what I was going through, yet when I told her, it felt better to relieve some of the pain that I was enduring.

Maybe it won't be so different?

"Growing up wasn't really easy for me. Let's just say that my childhood has been filled with events pertaining to being sexually assaulted and abused by the hands of my father. Although my mom has not *exactly* done anything to harm me, my father had left a mark on my mentality. But again, this has all been done in the past, and I just want to move forward in my life without carrying the damage," I said while wiping away my tears like windshield wipers were to sweep away the rain.

"I'm so sorry," Mr. Murray said.

"No need to apologize," I said while holding my hand up, knowing all too well of the phrase.

It was a moment of quietude before one of us could muster up the courage to break the silence.

"I understand how you feel. My sister used to have trouble coping with something she went through too. More along the lines of your situation, but different in a way."

My ears perked up.

"Really?" I said.

"Indeed," Mr. Murray said.

"How did she cope?"

Mr. Murray had spun around in his chair to face his beloved chalkboard.

As he got up from his leather chair, he wrote an eleven lettered word that I would not have cared to give my two cents for a thought.

When he was finished writing the word, he turned to me and wiped the chalk dust off his hands.

I kept rereading the word over and over again, hoping that it wouldn't have to come to this.

I expected that if I read it even more that it would compensate for the thought of doing it.

But the more I read the word, the more I realized I had to do it.

I looked to Mr. Murray, who had once shown me concern, now all willingly has hope that I will follow through.

"How could I do that?"

"You must allow yourself to before you can officially move on from this point."

I read the word again.

In his perfect cursive was the word that I couldn't care to believe in, let alone would not have believed in doing it myself.

Forgiveness.

"Nothing more, nothing less." Mr. Murray stated.

CHAPTER FIVE
Once a Hero, Now a Villain.

I grew up to love fairy tales.

I loved being able to read all the fairy tales that had a good ending to the story but was still hopeful that there was no end to the tale—always wondering if their life had turned out for the better after the pages had come to an end.

But what I never saw coming was how a beloved hero could easily come to be a spoiled apple of a villain.

He wasn't always a villain.

"*Now that you have your oval, you have to draw out the wings,*" he said.

The backyard had smelled of fresh mowed grass and flowers that had filled the air with its pollen. The bees were buzzing, the birds were chirping, and the sky had become clear of its clouds of gray. Although there was a fence that surrounded the perimeter of the yard, the neighbors were never shy to wave "hello" or a simple "goodbye." It was as if I was living in a utopia, and there was nothing to be wrong with the surroundings around me.

"*See! Nothing is hard if you just put your mind to it,*" he said.

My father and I were sitting on the porch of the back patio, drawing simple little butterflies that danced around each other in perfect harmony. He thought that it was time for his six-year-old daughter to begin the drawing lessons that he bragged about being the best of any arts and crafts activities.

"*What do you mean… I suck at this!*" I said while reluctantly giving off an overload of attitude for a six-year-old.

My father laughed jokingly and then looked at me with a sour face.

"*It doesn't look bad. You just need some more practice,*" he said, as he started shading in the shadows of one of the butterflies.

The butterflies he drew were absolutely breathtaking. The depth, shadows, the whole abstract of his drawings were remarkable. It was something that was embedded in my mind forever. His drawing was something that I knew I had looked up to.

If anything, it was my father who I looked up to the most.

I squinted back at my drawing, trying my hardest to see what my father had seen in the squiggly lines that held no form of a butterfly, just a blob. As my father continued to carefully shade and erase, I set aside the paper and pencil.

I got up and began to dance on the patio. Not just any dancing, but I started to waltz to the music that I knew no one could hear. As I danced, I closed my eyes and let my imagination run wild.

I visualized a room with crystal chandeliers dangling in a row upon the ceiling, showing off the most twinkling illumination. The walls were of a cream color that accented the framework of the most exhilarating gold leafing covering every inch of the walls. The floor was a light brown that was topped off with some sort of a gloss, giving the impression of shininess. As I had taken in the beauty of the room, I soon came to realize that I was standing in a ballroom.

When I felt the music come to a stop, a mirror had been set against the cream-colored wall compiled with gold leafing.

I had seen myself staring at the mirror in something that I thought I couldn't dream of wearing.

I saw myself in a poofy yellow dress that was layered so elegantly. It was as if the seamstress knew exactly how to flatter the eyes of any beholder. Upon the upper half of the yellow dress had laid crystals, letting the light be able to hit them with the most iridescent sparkle to the layered yellow dress.

As I was delicately fiddling with the dress, I heard a thud coming from behind.

I saw my father standing in a blue prestige tailcoat jacket that had a metallic gold lining, satin lapels, and buttons that had been placed in the center front of the suit. No longer was he wearing his casual clothing of an oversized red Nirvana shirt and baggy blue jeans.

The fairy tale that I grew to love came true, and I was briefly living in it.

"Would you care to dance, m'lady?" My father said as he closed the distance between him and I.

As he stood before me, he jokingly bowed before picking me up and spinning me in the air.

By the time we had tired ourselves out through our parade of steps and spins, we had sat down on the floor of the ballroom.

"For an old man, you're pretty good at dancing." I gave a smile that couldn't be mistaken for anything but zeal.

My father chuckled.

From what seemed like hours, my imagination began to come to a dim when I finally became aware of my father and I sitting on the lawn of our backyard.

Suddenly, I wasn't able to hear the symphonic buzzing of the bees or see the birds chasing after one another seamlessly nor smell the pollen that polluted the air. The sky above was now a charcoal black. As for now, the time had slipped through my little fingers, and the daylight had *been replaced with nighttime. The sky above held little spectacles that shed glimpses of light upon the dark, eerie night. The moon was placed in the essence of the sky and was comforted by the night's little spectacles that are known as stars.*

"Dad?" I looked at my father, whose gaze was fixed on the view above.

"Yes, pumpkin?" Still looking at the sky, he smiled.

I looked around in the midst of the night.

The tranquility of nightfall was not only relaxing but also peaceful.

"I wish we could stay like this forever," I said as I resumed to watch the night's withholding beauty.

Just when I thought nothing could come to be in the still of the darkness, a flash of pure light leaped before the stars and the moon.

"Woah, what was that? And where did it go?" Startled, I smiled and quivered with excitement.

My father smiled. "That was a shooting star. When you see a shooting star, you make a wish, and it'll come true."

I tightly closed my eyes shut and wished for the moment with my father would last forever. When I made a wish upon the shooting star, I looked to my father, who opened his eyes.

"Did you make a wish too?" I squealed.

"Mhmm." My father nodded his head.

"Well, what was it?"

My father then looked at me. His dark-brown eyes held my reflection, a child with so much hope for what only she had easily believed in.

"I wished that I could make this moment last longer for you." He said.

At that moment in my life, I couldn't foresee anything bad happening to me. As a child, I didn't need to worry about what precautions one would have to take. I believed that every occurrence that I was living in or even encountered, nothing bad would come of it.

My imaginative, creative mind was consistently enacting as the wheels of my fantasy.

My father was never to be the one to demolish the great high hopes and dreams for oneself—especially me. My father was the one to be an aspiration for amazing qualities through his endless actions. Nonetheless, he was my hero whom I idolized dearly.

My father was a hero.

Now he was disguised as a hero but had the intentions of that of a villain.

But, of course, only I would know that now.

CHAPTER SIX
Blackout.

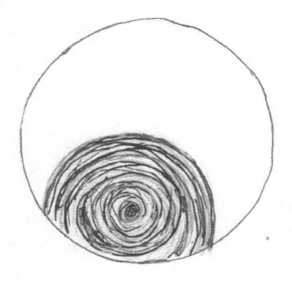

It was close to eleven at night, and my mind was racing.

I couldn't escape what Mr. Murray had said.

It was as if my mind was replaying the same scene repeatedly—Mr. Murray telling me that *forgiveness* would play a major role on a journey for me to heal.

It felt like my teacher had left me to solve a problem without guidance nor instructions on how to end up with the correct answer.

But who was I to kid?

Even if Mr. Murray was to tell me how to fully heal without forgiveness, there would still be an underlying gut feeling still present that my wounds still wouldn't be cured.

Why would I want to forgive my deadbeat of a father?

How was I supposed to come to terms with being able to let go of all the tormenting pain that was inflicted on me at such a young age—to be able to think of my father without recalling all the little hurtful details that made my childhood memories more daunting after the next.

Why should I be the bigger person?

I don't understand why I need to be the one to forgive someone who has done nothing but bring cruelty upon an innocent child, a child who was far beyond cleanhanded and gullible to believe she could trust the one person who she looked up to the most.

How could I come to forgive someone who should put aside their ego and admit their wrongdoing?

After all the reluctant battling with myself, why should I be the one to come forth and do the bidding?

Shouldn't the guilty have enough guilt to come clean to the innocent?

If anything, why should the innocent be left with nothing but compensation to grant amnesty to the guilty? Why should I be expected to follow through with forgiveness if he hasn't made any effort to come forth?

As my head was resting on the arm of the couch, the television's volume steadily increased—drowning my conflicting thoughts. I opened my eyes to see my mom standing above me, staring at the wide screen with the remote in her hand.

"Gosh, we need a new TV! I can barely hear it," Helen said.

As I sat up on the couch, I turned my head to look at my mom. With each step she took back to the kitchen, her long blonde curls would easily bounce off one another with ease. The way she glided with each step she took was as if she was on a runway. My mom had an outstanding body shape that could only be attained by working out a lot, which she never did.

How is it that someone who carries incredible genes gives birth to someone like me?

"Oh… I didn't know you were home," I said.

My mom stopped in her tracks and looked back at me with annoyance.

"Why wouldn't I be?" Helen's hand was on her hip as she began tapping her foot against the wooden floor of the kitchen. With each tap of her foot, I could only imagine the heat rolling off her shoulders.

"It's just that you are never here. You just caught me by surprise…" I said as I was beginning to feel squirmish.

As if hurt from what I said, she took her hand off her hip and folded her arms tightly close to her.

"Wow, after everything I have done for you, you repay me with insults under my own roof," Helen said.

"No, I didn't mean—"

My mom cut me off by raising her hand as if signaling for me to stop talking.

"Oh, I know *exactly* what you meant. Ever since your brother had left to go away for college, you've been nothing but complicated. Nonetheless, you have been such a pain to even deal with. Sometimes, you make living with you so hard and frustrating to the point where I wish I never had you!" The anger rolled off her shoulders, relieving the exasperation by her slouching her shoulders after spitting every hurtful word at me and sighing with relief.

Is this what she had really thought of me?

I never thought that someone who I had wanted to rekindle my relationship with would be this hurtful. But truth be told, have I really been so arrogant to dwell in my own turmoil to notice that I have been so hard to deal with?

I couldn't help but squint my eyes at not only the rash thought that I could possibly make someone feel this way about me but also the chance of not having the right moment to begin to have a relationship with my own mother.

"Would you just stop, Cadence? You always need to make everything about you," my mom spoke as she started to rub her temples.

With my index finger, I swiped away the tears that were running a marathon down the sides of my face.

"Instead, why don't you just go somewhere and take the crying with you?"

"Bu-u-t I ha-v-e nowh-er-e to go," I said, trying to speak calmly and clearly from my hysterical hyperventilating.

As if she had pitched to the catcher on the field, she whipped her keys to her fiery red Pontiac Grand Prix.

"Find somewhere to go." Helen said.

As the tears had quickened their pace, I hurried toward the front door with only my Converse on and no coat to shield me in the winter cold.

With the start of the engine, I slipped into the realization of isolation. I had no one.

Even though I had the comfort from Lance, who was miles away, Genevieve, who I could've easily called and talked to, there was no way out of feeling the bitter cold touch of hands that isolation placed on my shoulders.

I couldn't help but hear the lonesome muttering that isolation whispered in my ears, saying, *"You belong to me, or you are nothing but a vacant space, like me."*

With every inhale, I found it harder for me to breathe.

Why do I feel so alone?

As I backed out of the driveway, I turned on the heat in hopes of giving me warmth, as well as hoping that it will enable me to breathe a little easier.

I drove off.

I didn't care where I was going.

I just drove.

I could easily recall every word that Helen had said to me,

"I wish I never had you.
I wish I never had you.
I wish I never had you.
I wish I never had you.
I wish I never had you.
I wish I never had you."

My thoughts were beginning to trail off as the wheel had a mind of its own—to the left, to the right, now in the other lane.

Everything was beginning to become a blur as my eyes were patiently collecting the tears that were waiting for an out. Although the road was clear of its winter snow and ice, I could only see the pavement markings and traffic signals in sight.

Like my mind, the roads were deserted.

I find it hard to believe that even the ones that I try to hold dearest to me would believe the same things that I believed in myself.

Now all I could think of was how the back burner was starting to ignite.

I held onto the anger and confusion against my father, trying to make sense of how he could cause me to feel like I matter to no one, like how I didn't matter to him.

The back burner was hissing of heat, as it was now hoping that the light bulb would go off in my mind.

I swerved in the lane, causing the car to shift into the right lane.

Although I couldn't agree more with the idea of what the back burner held, how could I?

It was something that was considered a rash decision.

What if I regret it?

Not knowing what would be in store for me after this life had come to an end was scary.

I knew my destination was unclear, but it wouldn't matter anyway.

No one would even acknowledge that I would be gone.

Even Helen wouldn't notice.

Before I knew it, the wheel decided to make the decision for my fate.

I couldn't help but gain more dizzy as my peripheral vision was in the midst of being distorted by flying vivid colors. The wheel whipped the car to do a complete 360 along the road, spinning the car to a halt to land in the middle of a four-way intersection.

When the car came to a stop in the middle of the intersection, my forehead banged against the front dash—causing me to lose my focus, and that's when everything was slowly dimming into darkness.

Inhale. Exhale.

How am I alive?

I was lying on my back on something that felt prickly to the touch, but cool against my skin.

I opened my eyes.

The sky held an exotic variety of colors and the most exhilarating eye-catching birds flying through the air—birds that were to be seen from various locations from all over the world but came together in this very place to fly along the skyline.

Among the treetops, the birds flew as the sun peered through the branches of the trees.

Where am I?

I sat up to find me sitting on a patch of grass in a sheer white nightgown that flowed below my knees but just above my ankles.

I looked up from the nightgown and looked around me.

I was surrounded by tall aspen trees with the leaves sprouting brilliantly different colors of orange and green, and its bark was roughly laid on top of one another—showing not only its color of bark to be black but white as well. To the left of me, there was a breathtaking meadow with a magnificent vista of flowers—buttercups, docks, plantains, vetches, self-heals, scabiouses, dandelions, oxeye daisies, cowslips, and other unidentified plants. To the right of me, the trees formed along the sides of a gigantic pool of water, which depths seemed to be endless. Above the pool of water was an enormous hill of rock that could easily be mistaken for being ancient, for the rocks were beautifully worn down but strong nevertheless. The hill of rock carried the water down into the depths of the clear pool, flowing calmly as water clashed with water.

Around the hill of rock were tree branches that dangled above the glimmering pool of water, dancing to every beat the wind carried.

Inhale. Exhale.

The sunlight that had peered through the treetops now directed its light onto the peak of the waters, showing off the most spectacular scenery no mankind could imagine.

My body was quick to pick itself up and make its way toward the view.

As I had come close to the water, I had noticed a cement bench hidden within the grass that sat in front of the water.

I closed my eyes.

How am I still able to breathe? I would think that after the chaotic spin of the car and thunk of a head, it would be good enough to be rid of my ability to breathe, so why didn't it?

"Cadence."

Startled at the sound of my name, I opened my eyes to see a man standing in front of me. The man was dressed in a white robe, had brown hair, and stunning emerald eyes. In the presence of this man, I couldn't be more than confused as to how I felt the need to not be startled.

"W-who are you?" *I asked.*

"You don't know me, but I know you," *the man said with confidence, as he had taken the initiative to sit by me on the cement bench.*

"You have grown so much...but you're not allowing yourself to continue to grow if you still deny yourself to break free of the chains you possess," *the man stated.*

I glanced at the man.

"I don't understand..." *I said as the man looked at me and smiled.*

"Those chains that you drag, are your pain. You have done nothing but gain more tired after all the hauling you do."

I looked away from the man.

How could this man know of anything of what I am going through, let alone tell me something that I already knew?

"Cadence," *the man spoke politely.*

I turned my head to see his gaze was focused on the pool of water that sat in front of us.

There on the shallow end of the water stood a little girl who was dancing and splashing around in the water. The little girl had a caramel complexion, brown curly hair, and an adorable smile. This little girl was dressed as if she was the flower girl at a wedding, wearing a cute white dress that's poofy but looked absolutely adorable on her.

"That was you." *The man chuckled.*

"What do you mean?" *I questioned.*

"This was a version of yourself before your father had chosen a different path—before he whispered in your ears of the horrible things he could do, took away your innocence, made you feel worthless, made you feel like you aren't beautiful, unleashed his anger on you. After all that happened, and you are still reliving in pain. You were once so happy,"

Like on repeat, my tears slipped away before I could try to hold them back.

"I know that you also share a complicated relationship with your mother, but that's something that you seem to not let bother you as much—more like you seem to hold a grudge more against your father than you would your mother, and I can understand why. You held more of a relationship with your father than you had with your mother before he was corrupted."

"How do you know about this? All of it?" I wiped away the tears and stiffened up.

"Like I said, I know you," he calmly spoke.

I rose from the cement bench and walked closer to the little girl who continued to splash and play on the shore of the water.

The little girl became aware of my distance and looked up at me with admiration.

"Hi! I'm Cadence." She smiled and reached out to take my hand.

"W-well, hi," I said, as I was crying uncontrollably inside, behind the faint smile I held.

The little girl then took my hand and placed it on her cheek and looked up at me once again.

I couldn't help but envy this little girl.

She was the little girl who had so much to offer the world with her creativity, love, innocence, and light.

The little girl had everything I wished I did.

Now that little girl was no longer real.

She had died a long time ago with what she once knew—all that is lost now.

The little girl removed my hand and backed away slowly.

Her once known light was starting to dim and fade away.

"No! Please! Stay!" I yelled at the top of my lungs while trying to grab onto anything I could of her.

The little girl's presence evaporated among the scent of fresh water I once wanted to breathe in.

Now it's as if the air was filled with poison.

It was beginning to get harder for me to breathe.

I collapsed on the solid ground.

I wept as loud as a widow and felt nothing more than loss itself.

"You were so happy," the man said, as he stood hovering over me.

Staring at the ground, the grass could be seen covered by the dirt. The dirt had taken up so much of the grass, that the grass wasn't able to overgrow the dirt.

I raised my head and looked up at the man.

"Why? You had multiple opportunities to intervene when things had not continued to get better, and you did nothing. Nothing. As if I wasn't worthy of being saved from the disasters that you knew about. How come if you knew me, you couldn't save me?" I screamed as my tears were overflowing into a puddle.

The man smiled.

Even with my yelling, the man couldn't show any signs of anger or even disinterest.

"If I had intervened, then you would not have gained any experience in what life has to offer. No matter what anyone goes through, life is hard. Those who are given more of a difficult route are those who are strong enough to conquer what suffering they had endured. It's only up to those who face hard times to declare what they are going to make of it," the man said.

"But I am not strong. I am on the verge of removing myself from every equation. I am on the verge of losing my sanity." I wept.

The man had knelt to my level and took both of my hands.

"You are made to do great things, Cadence. You are not a mistake, nor will you ever be. Your worth has not diminished. You still have more to give than you can imagine. You may have suffered tribulation in your past, but that does not mean you still have to suffer now. If anything, your sanity is in the palm of my hands." The man held so much compassion in his eyes and sincerity in his tone of voice.

"Please…help me," I cried out.

The man smiled and placed his right hand in the middle of my chest.

In an instant, I felt all the pain that I was so consumed with leaving my body and diving straight into the palm of his hand.

My crying slowly began to resolve, as I had felt that there was no reason to cry now.

The pain that had tormented me, the pain that had oppressed me for all these years was now gone.

"B-but how?" I said.

The man gave me another smile.

"Know that you are no longer in the shackles that you have carried with you everywhere you went. Do not hold grudges to those who have hurt you, for it will only bring you agony." The man arose, bringing me up with him.

"But how?" I said once more.

"You will know soon enough." The man turned his back and started to walk away.

"I don't want to be alone again. Please come back!"

The man stopped and turned to look back at me for the last time.

"You are never alone, for I will always be with you."

In a flash, darkness had come to veil everything in sight.

"Helen! She's awake!"

As if my eyes were glued shut, I slowly pried them open with a few blinks.

"Ouch," I said as my head was pounding as hard as a drum.

When I opened my eyes, Genevieve had let go of my hand, and Helen rushed in through the door.

"Ugh, where am I?" I sat up.

"You're in the hospital, Cadence. Do you remember what happened?" Helen said with concern.

Despite my shock of how concerned Helen was, how couldn't I remember it all?

"Yes, and I am so sorry for causing a catastrophe for you." No matter what my mom and I have gone through with one another, I felt sorry for causing all of this—everything.

"You're fine, sweetheart. I'm going to go get the doctor so that he is aware that you are awake! Be right back." Helen smiled and hurried out the door.

"Did I miss something? Since when did she ever call me, *sweetheart?*" I giggled as I looked at Genevieve.

For the first time ever, Genevieve stared back at me, conveying no emotion.

"Since you were in a coma for three months," Genevieve said, as she grabbed a tissue that was waddled up in her pocket and wiped her face from any preexisting trails of tears.

I didn't know what was more bizarre, that I have been in the hospital for three months or that something *happened* while I was in this "coma."

"Oh," I said.

"How do you feel?" Genevieve asked.

"I feel better, believe it or not. But something happened to me during the time I was in a coma. There was this man, and he had shown me so many things that I wouldn't think would be possible," I said. "The man knew *everything* about me."

Genevieve tilted her head, trying to think of what in the world I was talking about.

"Are you sure you're okay?" Genevieve rested the back of her hand on my forehead, checking to see if the delusional nonsense could be explained.

My gaze turned from Genevieve as I removed her hand from my forehead.

I sighed and rested my hand on my chest, feeling the rise and fall of my breathing.

Taken aback, the dream I had while I was in this coma didn't feel like a dream. If anything, it felt like it was a calling—an awakening.

It felt like it was my reality, that I needed to make a change.

The need that I felt after waking up from it was unreal, the need that I didn't need to drag the ongoing pain—that I could actually be happy for once.

Beyond everything, I couldn't have gotten to this point without that man who made his appearance known to me in my reality.

The gratitude that I had come to feel for someone whose name I didn't even catch was more than I could ever express.

I couldn't help but be left with unanswered questions.

I couldn't help but wonder why he had done me a favor by taking all of what had resided within me.

I couldn't help but smile.

CHAPTER SEVEN
Male Figure, Brother, and a Best Friend.

Never had Lance failed to not only protect me from any harm that may have come my way but was also always there when I needed him.

Growing up, we both always thought we could rely on a stable family but never believed we could get that in return.

Although we shared the same mother, we didn't share the same father.

Our fathers were constantly in and out of our lives, but when they did make an appearance, we always welcomed them back with open arms.

How could anyone blame us?

Throughout everything that I had faced alone, I had liked to believe that no matter what, I had Lance there to comfort me, whether he was aware of the comfort I was in need of or just being the big brother that I knew he was capable of being.

"Get out," my father said sternly, as I held my breath in and scavenged for the handle to get out of the car. As I shut the door to the dirt brown 2000 Chevrolet Silverado, I could hear the rust meet against the wintery snow that had laid among the pavement of my driveway.

While walking up to the house, all I could see was the icicles that were slowly beginning to drip off the edge of the rooftop. Michigan's winter was always dreadful, but somehow the wind had held more warmth to it than it had usually did.

As I opened the door to my house, I saw Lance sitting on the couch, surfing through different channels.

"Hey, Cad!" Lance said, smiling as if he hadn't seen me in ages.

I gave him a smile back and shut the door behind me.

"Mom isn't here?" I said.

"Nope," he stated.

I put my backpack filled with my clothes by the door and plopped down right next to Lance on the couch.

Instead of cruising through the channels, Lance turned off the television and turned to face me.

"How was your Dad's? I haven't seen you since Friday. Tell me all about it," Lance said while nodding his head as a cue for me to tell him about my visit.

No one knew of what happened behind closed doors, and the fear that overcame me of telling the truth wasn't worth it.

I was always petrified of telling anyone.

Besides the threats coming from that of my father, I had seemed to accept the truth that no one would believe me anyway.

"It was good. We went to the movies, and we played some new games on his PlayStation four," I said, hoping that my little white lies were not to be seen through.

"That really sounds like fun. I wish I was there!" He said.

"Trust me, so do I."

Lance got up and went to the kitchen.

"So what do you want to eat for dinner?" Lance asked.

I looked at the kitchen stove and noticed the time was already five thirty.

"Do you know where Mom went?" I asked in curiosity.

Lance looked at me and then gave his apologetic look.

"I'm not sure where she is right now. The last time I saw her, it was the day before you left. She didn't tell me where she went or how long she'll be."

My brother was among a few that could tell me the most dreadful news, and I could still feel at ease.

Even though my brother was only a year older than I was, I knew he was capable of handling a young kid at home by himself. The appreciation that I had for him could go on without being said because, at the end of the day, he was the one who I came home to every day.

Lance and I never really had any supervision on weekdays after school or even the weekends. Our mom really had not seen any point in having a babysitter. All she would say is "Why should I waste my time? You guys can watch yourselves."

And that's what we did.

My mom, Lance, and I never had any family members who were worth counting on. Basically, our entire family had been really distant from my mom. No one wanted to trap themselves in the web of Helen or the responsibilities she had owned up to—but didn't want to take care of.

It had always been my mom, Lance, and I.

More like Lance and I.

Helen had always chosen the wrong activities to occupy the time she had when she wasn't home with us or whenever she wasn't working. She had found herself in the strangest bars with her group of friends, drinking away time as it flew by. She had always wandered the empty houses of her one-night stands when the family was away. She even sometimes slept in her fiery red Pontiac Grand Prix, knowing all too well she would get neck cramps from sleeping so uncomfortably. Whether she would come home drunk with her friends accompanying her, coming home looking as ruffled as a dog or not even coming home nights on end.

Lance and I knew all too well of what she was up to.

No doubt in my mind that I had always yearned for a relationship with Helen, but I could never seem to spark an interest in her eyes.

"What is there to eat?" I spoke optimistically.

Lance looked in the pantry and then the fridge.

The pantry had begun to be consumed by the cobwebs, as it had barely any canned goods or even food present. The fridge was in the midst of smelling like something had a traumatic death and stayed put in the same spot for hours without being attended to.

"I think I just lost my appetite," I muttered underneath my breath in disgust.

"Me too." Lance took a couple of steps back and closed the door to the fridge.

I then went to lie on the couch, hoping that Helen would come back home. Lance sat down next to my head and began to play with my hair, letting each strand of my hair be able to get a chance to be entwined with a different strand by its overdirection.

As Lance played with my hair, I fell into a deep sleep.

Helen was rarely home, but Lance was always home.

Out of the four seasons, winter was by far my favorite.

So many people would look at winter being the most horrendous season of them all. Winter to people would be described as cold, freezing rain, slippery roads, snowstorms, or even hell on Earth. But what people cannot foresee is the beauty that is held within each snowflake, each breathtaking snowman, and the glistening snow that sparkled underneath the sun's rays.

So many people have the capability to dismiss the fact that there is hidden beauty just beyond the surface.

Winter was amazingly beautiful beyond what most could see.

As the snowflakes were falling gracefully to the ground, I began to combine the snow to create the second part of my snowman. I gathered smooth black rocks from the flowerbeds by the house and had them enact as buttons on the second part of the snowman. Once I had the base and the second part of the snowman together, I formed the head. With some black rocks, a black beanie hat, and an unusually small carrot, the snowman was complete. As I stepped back to observe my creation, Lance came out from the house and stood on the patio.

"I think you forgot something, Cad!" Lance yelled from the patio all the way to the backyard.

I looked back to the snowman and saw nothing out of sorts.

The snowman was perfect!

Lance then ran down the downward slope of a hill, trying his best not to trip among the glistening snow, to run to the big oak tree that stood firm in the sky.

Like a snap of the wrist, Lance broke off two twigs of the big oak tree.

"What's a snowman without arms?" Lance chuckled.

I smiled and placed the two twigs from the big oak tree on the sides of the snowman.

"Now he is complete!" I said.

"Here, I made you something." Lance pulled out his one-of-a-kind stainless steel thermos container out of his hoodie and handed it to me.

As my anticipation exceeded, I opened it and smelled heaven for the first time in forever.

"Hot chocolate! Mhmm, thank you, Lance!"

Lance smiled at me and then looked back at my snowman.

"Promise me something, Cad."

As I gulped down the hot chocolate, I looked at Lance in concern.

"Yes, Lance?" I said dim-wittedly.

"No matter what you face in life, whether I am by your side or not, you need to have the dedication to stay as true to yourself as you possibly can. You have so much potential and good to do in the world, and I don't want you to think for a split second that you don't have anything to offer to anyone or anything. Yeah, things may be rough around the edges as of the moment, but that doesn't mean that you are any less of having an amazing future ahead of you. You are a brilliant, optimistic, caring, adventurous person. Not only are you all these things, but also, you are my sister—most importantly, my best friend. So please don't lose sight of what I see."

I set the thermos onto the ground and gave Lance the biggest hug I could offer to anyone.

In the winter cold, I found not only a male figure to whom I could look up but also I found a protective brother and a caring best friend.

CHAPTER EIGHT
Truth Be Unraveled.

I feel like time has stolen some of the most precious moments that I was so blind to notice.

Although I was stuck between intervals, time had flown by.

The hospital was loud and obtained such a unique smell to it that others would twitch their noses in disgust. The distinctive setting had no impact on my continuous thoughts that couldn't help but wander.

After the crash, I felt like I was in a dream, a dream where I wasn't familiar with my surroundings and could easily recognize the beauty behind the scenery that men had not corrupted. Even though it had felt like a dream, it felt as if it was my reality, a reality that was coincidental to what the very most thing that I was bonded by. Everything about this occurrence was absolutely breathtaking, but then at the near end, everything became unclear.

There was this man.

Disregarding me being around the opposite gender that usually had stirred discomfort within me, the man that mysteriously appeared out of thin air had a sense of hospitality to his aura. Just to be in his presence seemed like he knew me before even meeting me. Like he knew every detail there was about me, including everything that I was put through.

Through and through, I felt the love that overflowed from his presence. The love that had filled every part of my being was enough to be said.

I no longer felt victimized.

I no longer could feel like the torment that sufficed me.

In this particular moment of meeting this man, he never introduced himself to me—not one name or clue as to who he was. Yet when I woke up, I believed that there must be something more to the man's identity. This again, leaving my thoughts to wander to the strenuous possibilities that one could develop a headache when overthinking.

Besides everything that had occurred within this reality, I never got the chance to thank the man for what he had done.

"You know, you should really eat, Cadence," Helen said.

From the ceiling, I looked at what was placed in front of me.

There was a brown plastic tray that was holding what the hospital called *food*—red jiggly Jell-O, flimsy green broccoli, and brown moldy meat loaf.

I lightly pushed the tray away from my view, still distracted from the thoughts that kept bombarding my mind.

"I'm not really hungry," I said.

Helen was leaning up against the wall of the room in her light-blue scrubs that were already wrinkled from worry.

"Cadence, I…" She began to say, then she looked down to the left of her like she was holding back something that she had wanted to say, but she couldn't.

Without her even needing to say the words that I knew she couldn't begin to say out loud, I looked to her with compassion.

"I know."

Helen rose her head and wiped away what had seemed to be something that I have never seen on her before.

Trying to dismiss the silence, I quietly cleared my throat.

"I should probably head home right now and get ready for work," Helen said as she swiftly moved toward the open door.

"Before I leave, there are a few people who would like to speak to you," Helen said.

Standing by the door, Helen waved her hand for whoever it was to come into the room.

"Hey, Cad."

There he stood with his hands in his pockets with beady red eyes and smiling so fondly like he found what he was looking for.

"Lance!" Almost jumping out of the hospital bed, I excitedly put my hands to my face in shock.

Without me needing to get up out of bed, he ran to my bedside and embraced me in a welcoming hold.

With heavy breaths, I could sense Lance smiling into my shoulder as I stiffened at the intensity of his embrace.

"I thought I wouldn't be able to see you again," Lance said as he pulled back.

As he was implying something more, the sight of Lance was nothing but worrisome.

To see him in pain was as if I was in pain.

"I'm sorry," I apologetically spoke.

"No, you have no reason."

"But I—" As I was about to reason with him, he placed his hands on mine and looked up at me with the most sincerity written across his face.

"I'm just glad that you are okay," Lance said.

The very essence of the underlying truth that had been swept under the rug was one of the very few things that had kept me from being okay.

How could I be okay?

I exhaled long and slow until Lance and I heard two hard knocks at the door. No longer was Helen standing near the door, but instead, there was Genevieve holding a brown paper bag in her right arm.

Lance moved away from me and sat in one of the isolated green leather chairs right beside me.

"Ahh, I was wondering where you went." I grinned.

Once I had awoken from what had been a reality, Genevieve was by my side. But a few moments went by, and the next thing I knew, she had vanished out of thin air.

"I went to go get you something," Genevieve stated as she placed the brown paper bag on my lap.

With no patience that held me back from opening the brown paper bag, I shred open to what was containing the prize inside.

With nothing covering the item, I held it up and examined the trinket.

It was a rectangular box with gray coating and dark-gray decor on the top of it, as there was a picture of a full moon with the words of *'I love you to the moon and back'* written on the side of the full moon.

"Open it." Genevieve clapped with her hands.

As I carefully began to open the box, it had started to play a sweet uplifting lullaby that could've easily rocked anyone to sleep on its own. On the right side of the music box, you could see the machinery that had made the box play a tune. Whereas on the left side, there was a little brown package sitting in the designated placement for anyone to put their jewelry, etc. in. I revealed the small package to Genevieve in confusion and amusement.

"Yes, open it."

Lightly, I made a rip in the package. As I tore the package open, I uncovered a silver chain necklace that had held a vertical-shaped pendant that said *"warrior"* on it with a tiny outline of a heart at the very end of the word.

"It is so beautiful, Genevieve," I squealed as I put the necklace and music box close to my chest.

"The music box is from mom and me," Lance spoke. "But I had no clue about the necklace." Lance gave a death glare at Genevieve, who was still glancing my way.

"You're welcome." She smiled.

Without Genevieve needing to tell me of why she had decided to get this for me, I then had a feeling kick me in the gut for what only I could know that it was time.

I set aside the music box and put on the necklace that I was beginning to adore. As I heard the clasp of the necklace click, I rubbed my index finger against the engravement of the word *warrior*.

Never had I gained the perspective of being able to see myself as a warrior. I always thought that what I had gone through in the past was something that I wasn't able to fight through or even muster up the bravery to fight against.

It was hard for me to see myself as someone who was still able to get up in the morning and pretend as if nothing had happened the previous day. Entirely unaware, I was fighting the oppression that had me unable to move mentally.

The torture that I felt that I needed to abide by because I was scared for my own survival. The fear that tapped on my shoulder to wake me in the night felt as if I needed to have the bravery to do what had been asked of me to survive.

I was a warrior who knew one thing, survival.

I was so overwhelmed by what I had gone through that it had mentally put me in a place to where I couldn't even subside the thoughts that distorted my sense of laughter and my carefree ways—that a child could maintain until they grew older.

I was damaged, fighting a brawl that I didn't choose to fight in.

Therefore, I was a warrior who others didn't know of.

The hospital's visiting hours were soon coming to an end, as I still wanted to engage in the various conversations that had made me overfill with joy as I was surrounded by my favorite two people.

"Ugh, why can't we stay here all night?" Lance chuckled, as we had just finished talking about how crazy and wild Lance's stay at college was.

"Because they're the rules, and rules need to be followed," Helen said as she closed the door behind her.

Helen was dressed in her usual light-blue scrubs, along with her name badge and her stethoscope.

"You guys should probably get going though. If not, the security guards might throw you out." Helen chuckled.

When Lance and Genevieve started to put on their coats, I looked down at the necklace Genevieve gave me.

The reminder that I had been putting off until the right moment had come to present itself.

"Uhm, before you all go, there is something that I want to tell you guys," I spoke aloud.

As Genevieve and Lance stopped to put their coats on and Helen ceased to walk toward the door, they all looked at me and waited for me to speak.

"I have had a hard time coming to terms with everything that has happened to me, and I am not just talking about this *accident* that had just happened." As I continued, Helen and Lance came closer to me as Genevieve stood in front of me with a facial expression that only I would be able to understand.

"Growing up, I had been taken advantage of and abused by Leavan, under the noses of countless people, including you guys. He would threaten me to not speak a word to another soul, as well as order me to do so many things that I couldn't imagine doing at such a young age," I said, as my tears were tired of being held back, and my voice began to shake.

"I tried so h-hard to get rid of the very things that had contaminated my own thoughts, to try to believe that I was more than something that couldn't be violated. All this time, I had thought of myself as an object that held no value and was nothing but damaged. And I'm so sorry that I couldn't have told you guys sooner. It-t's just that I was scared. *I am so scared*," I cried.

It felt like I was being eaten alive with everything that I tried to bury underneath the surface.

Helen was covering her mouth as if everything she was appalled by, as Lance was looking down at the ground.

"Why couldn't you come to me, Cad?" Lance questioned.

"I was scared no one would believe me, Lance.. I'm so sorry for not saying anything." I cried as I covered my face with the pillow behind me wiping away the tears that my eyes could no longer hold.

From the warmth of the hands that were placed on my right shoulder, I had seen tears sliding their way down Helen's face. Once I had felt another hand caress my left shoulder, I looked to Lance to see the support that I knew I could rely on.

"I believe you, Cadence." Genevieve spoke as she plopped on the hospital bed.

"I believe you, Cad." Lance said as he and Genevieve hugged me—making me the center of the group hug.

As Genevieve and Lance gave me a hug that was needed for so long, I felt the warmth of the hand on my right shoulder leave. From the tight opening gap in the group hug, I could see Helen exit the hospital room with her phone to her ear and could hear the worry stressed in her tone of voice.

CHAPTER NINE
The Loss of a Flower.

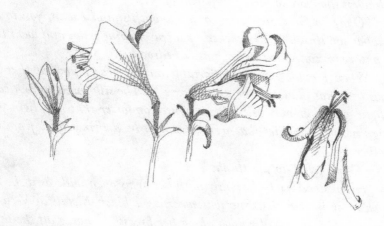

Undoubtedly, I loved my mom, and I knew that she loved me.

Yet sometimes, I would question the chance that her love would wither and die out—even if I knew better or not.

"Cadence, would you come here for a second?" Helen called out.

I was in the living room, coloring in the daisy flower that I drew the prior day, trying to the best of my ability to evenly shade within the boundaries of the lines.

While shading in the middle part of the daisy yellow, I slowly began to cease shading. When I laid the yellow colored pencil down alongside the drawing, I took in the beauty of what I was perceiving.

With each stroke of the colored pencil, I was able to create a black and white portrait, only to bring the portrait to life with the divinity of color.

As I picked myself off the ground, I made my way toward Helen's room, which had been enclosed in a dead-end hallway on the other side of the house.

"I need your help getting ready for a date," Helen stated as she was rummaging through her closet, throwing clothes onto the bed that she could foresee herself wearing.

"Who's the guy?" I questioned with curiosity.

"Mhmm, just a…friend." Helen smirked mischievously.

I couldn't help but become aware of how Helen was oddly selective with what she wore to meet this friend of hers.

"Okay, so I'm going to try on a few outfits, and I want you to tell me what you think." Helen picked up a few clothing items and went into the bathroom connected to her master bedroom.

When I made myself comfortable on the bed, I noticed that her sheets were not made of linen but pure silk. The silk sheets were a color of light gray that matched with a white comforter that had light gray designing of calla lilies that were shown to be drifting away from one another.

"Okay, what do you think?"

Helen stood back gloriously with her arms open wide as if she had no sway of insecurities. She was wearing a black Metallica V-cutout choker T-shirt that had ripples along her breasts, showing off the uttermost sight of her bosom. With her overbearing Metallica shirt, she wore black leggings with black Nike shoes.

Helen then walked in front of the huge rectangular mirror that had been attached to her dresser, looking at every feature she had possessed.

"So?" She asked as she was looking at her reflection, obviously talking to me.

"Uhhh, I don't know about that shirt," I stuttered.

Helen tossed her blonde curly hair onto her shoulders, fluffing the hair out as her eyes caught sight of her shirt in the mirror.

"Why not?" Helen said reluctantly.

"It shows this," I said, gesturing to my chest. "And I thought you were meeting a friend."

Helen turned to me and then choked on what had seemed to be a laugh.

"*Hunny, you don't have anything to show for up here,*" Helen touched her boobs and laughed with no control. "*You would think that you would've hit your grow spurt now that you're eleven.*"

I looked down.

My chest was as flat as a pancake. As Helen kept laughing, I folded my arms to cover my chest.

"*Okay, but seriously… I don't think it's bad. If anything, my friend will like what he sees,*" Helen said as she fixed her bra straps. "*I'm not sure if these are doing me any justice though. What do you think?*" She said, referring to her black skintight leggings and black Nike shoes.

"*Maybe jeans?*" I questioned.

Helen started to nod her head and smile vigorously.

"*Now we're talking! Let me see if I can find a pair,*" Helen said.

I began to feel more uncomfortable as I began to stir among the sheets.

I pushed the clothing away from me, making a clear space for any discomfort that would find ease from not being so claustrophobic.

As the bathroom door swung open, I saw Helen wearing light-blue jeans that had been torn and pried open above her knees and slightly below.

"*Uhm…*" Stunned by the appearance of my mom, I didn't know what to make of her choice of style.

"*Cute, huh?*" Helen smiled and went to the mirror to admire what I had been seeing.

"*Are you sure that this is…appropriate?*" I calmly questioned with uncertainty.

Helen turned her head in a fast motion to look at me with the most disinterested facial expression.

"*Really? I thought it made my butt look good,*" she said.

"*Mom,*" I said, following with an unapproved nod of the head.

"*You're just upset that you don't have anything to work with to flatter the boys of your own age. So don't try to put me down just because you weren't born with what I got,*" Helen said as she turned her gaze to look back in the mirror, picking up the lipstick and drawing it on her oversized lips.

I felt overly insecure of everything about myself, especially the way I looked.

I couldn't help but recognize the very few flaws that even my mom had taken into recognition. Soon I began to feel like those tiny flaws that Helen pointed out were astoundingly unfolding into the overall idea of myself.

I wasn't sure whether critiquing my body was for her own twisted pleasure or a way that she could tell me that I just wasn't good enough.

Either way, my mom's perspective on how she viewed her daughter was nothing but discouraging to my body image.

Without a word being said between the two of us, she made her way to the bed and sat right beside me, where I had cleared a spot free of clothing.

"You know when you meet a guy and you feel those butterflies in your stomach?" She spoke.

To make the conversation short, I agreed with her.

"Well, in order for that guy to feel those butterflies in his stomach, you have to simply dress to impress," Helen gestured to her outfit. "And this is how to impress."

I looked away from her.

How come I would need to wear such treacherous clothing, just to get a guy to notice me?

If anything, why would I go beyond measures to impress just one guy?

"So you like this friend?" I asked.

"Well, he's a special kind of friend," She swooned.

Helen took her arm and enveloped me into a fine hold.

"You see, when you meet a special friend, you have the opportunity to give them your flower." Helen slowly talked as if she were choosing her words carefully.

I looked back up at her.

"What do you mean, my flower?" I said, dumbfounded.

Helen shrugged her shoulders and chuckled to herself.

"Oh, little one...your flower is your virginity. Sex is something that you and someone special do that is very intimate. Once done for the first time, then you can never regain your flower back," Helen uttered.

"Well, where is the flower, and what is sex?" I whispered.

Helen removed her arm that kept me close to her and sat still beside me.

As if the conversation had made her uncomfortable, she looked like she was hesitant about the subject that she had started.

"I-it's this area," Helen pointed to the region down below.

"Sex is when you feel intimacy with your special friend, and you guys share that intimacy by doing grown-up things with one another in that area."

Following the point of her finger, I soon came to understand what she was talking about.

"But why do they call it a flower?" I questioned, divulging into the topic.

Helen was hesitant once again.

When she looked like she wanted to say something, she stopped herself and then rethought what the best possible response would be.

"Imagine you picked this beautiful lily flower that you saw in a garden, and you wanted to keep it. But once you do decide to have sex with your special friend, then that elegant lily is no longer beautiful. Your flower has been crushed and used." Helen exhaled a long breath as she got up. "I'm glad we got that conversation over and done with. Now go get ready for bed. Lance will be here in a few minutes from basketball practice. I'm gonna take off," Helen demanded as she grabbed her purse off from the dresser.

"But how—" I began to ask.

"No, that's enough. Go get ready for bed, now." Helen asserted.

I jumped from the bed and walked out.

The misconceptions that were running through my mind were countless.

It was as if I was exposed to something that I felt like I could've known but then realized it was something that I was never told before.

Why did this all seem familiar?

Was I experiencing some sort of déjà vu?

I went back into the living room, ignoring what Helen had asked of me, and proceeded to shade within the drawing of the daisy.

Even though I wanted to stop thinking of the possibility of losing my flower, I felt some part of me was missing.

The thought of me losing my flower was beginning to torment me. I had this gut-wrenching instinct that something wasn't right. Something that I thought was there wasn't—something that would not have been easily tricked, but allowed.

The thought of me giving this flower to someone who I didn't betroth it to nor didn't have any clue whatsoever of giving it to was like an itch under my skin.

I started thinking of how my father could've easily sworn off the confusion, but then it began to register that the feeling of losing something felt well known.

It was like the feeling had been present before, resurfacing to the top.

After that, I had forgotten the feeling, along with the memory. It all dawned on me.

"Lie down."

I trembled in worry at the sound of his raspy voice. I stumbled upon his bed and began to lie down next to him.

When I finally made myself comfortable on the edge of the bed, my father moved closer to me.

"Are you ready for your first lesson?" My father breathed in my ear.

I trembled at the thought of me, allowing this to give this up to him.

I hated myself for bestowing this token of innocence to him as if it was a reward.

I hated that I was tricked into believing that it was normal, that something of my own could easily have been fooled.

I hated myself for being fooled.

I once had my *flower.*

A *flower* that was once beautiful but now is crushed and used.

CHAPTER TEN
To Forgive But Never Forget.

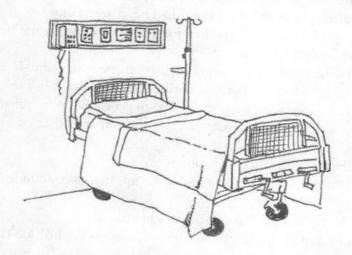

After waking up from what had been my reality, I made it aware to Helen, Lance, and Genevieve of what had been scratching every particle of my being for so long. Although Genevieve had already known, just her presence was enough for support.

I stayed in the hospital for a couple of days after waking up for the doctors wanted to run some tests and double-check my vitals once more before sending me back home.

"I can't believe you beat me again!" Helen cried out.

As I put the six dice back in the purple velvet baggie, I gave a victory smirk of a winner.

"Well, I guess that just shows you that you're just not that good at ten thousand." I shrugged.

I had never seen this version of my mom before. Prior to the accident, she was always distant. She never wanted to hangout. If she did, it was for her own selfish reasons.

Helen laughed as she got up from the isolated green chair that sat beside my bed and looked down at me.

"After I am finished with my shift, we're going home, and we'll do whatever you want tonight. Sounds like a plan?" Helen proposed.

I smiled and nodded my head in reply.

Helen smiled and then gave me a kiss on the forehead in response. As she made her way to exit the room, I noticed that she was radiating with this light that I had never seen before.

Once Helen left, I grabbed my phone that sat on the bedside table and called Genevieve.

As the phone rang, my anticipation grew exceedingly as my curiosity for what I had missed during the coma was only a few rings away. Just as the rings were continuing to get closer to the voice mail, I heard a distant voice mumble coming from the other end of the phone.

"Hey, it's Cadence!" I announced.

Though it was like she just woke up, her voice sounded a bit hazy.

"Hey-y, Cad. What's up?" She yawned.

I looked at the small black box that sat on the bedside table to see that it had digital numbers in neon green, seeing that it was only six o'clock in the morning.

"Sorry if I woke you up. I just wanted to talk to you before I got discharged," I sympathetically mentioned.

"No, you're fine! I was just about to get up." Genevieve yawned again as I heard rustling going on in the background.

"Okay," I said. "I wanted to ask you more about what had happened when I was, ya know…"

Just as it could be in person, there was a moment of stillness.

When I thought that the call had ended, she finally spoke up.

"It was really hard for all of us, Cadence. Even Mr. Murray came down to the hospital to check up on you," Genevieve uttered.

I had no idea of the severity of me being in this coma—that it would even cause my high school teacher to come down and see how I was doing.

To think that I thought no one had really cared for me.

"But what had exactly happened to my mom? Since when did she become this whole other person?" I asked.

"Honestly, Cadence…she was worse than any of us. We were told that you had suffered from a really bad traumatic brain injury from the accident, and that it was a possibility that you weren't going to wake up. The doctors had told her that it would be best for you and us if she made the decision to let you go. Sadly, a couple of weeks before you woke up, we all came to the conclusion that you weren't going to make it. The only one who didn't give up on you, was your mom. Your mom was heartbroken, Cadence. There would be moments where *I* had to be her shoulder to cry on because she had no one to lean on," she added.

Guilt had struck my heart.

How could I be this reckless?

But then again, I had no idea before that I was loved this much.

"I can't tell you how sorry I feel about causing you and everyone else to go through this much agony over me," I noted.

"There is nothing that you should feel sorry for, Cadence. Look, I have to get ready for school, but I'll text you later, okay?"

With uncertainty, I replied with an "okay."

When Genevieve hung up, I was still on the other line, over-thinking the whole thing that she had explained to me over the phone.

Despite the fact that I still feel guilty, I still felt that everything was my fault.

Before I could push the end call button, the phone had done me a favor by hanging up itself.

My room in the hospital had attained no company but my loneliness.

Although I told the people dearest to me what had happened between Leavan and me, I still felt like there was something holding me back. Even though the man in my reality had healed me in some way, I still felt as if I had work to do internally that was still holding a tight grip on me—like it still was controlling me.

I tilted my head back onto the pillow as I sighed and closed my eyes in defeat.

How could I be able to ever get past this?

Despite that I could barely feel the emptiness that had eaten me alive before, I noticed that I had a sense of purpose to be something more than what I had made myself as—to be rid of the feelings that had chained themselves to me for so long.

Besides feeling like I had this purpose, at the same time, I just wanted to give up on trying to get past what I had always known to feel. I put aside these emotions for some time now. Just to face them head-on is something that I wasn't really sure if I was strong enough to do. If I had some way to be able to get past everything that happened with Leavan, I would feel more free than imprisoned.

Was the chance to be free more attainable than caving into these emotions that have controlled the mentality that I grew to live by?

My thoughts were eroding with the chance that I wouldn't have to do either. That I wouldn't have to take the hard way to earn the freedom that I wanted or even easily cave into the feelings that had drowned me in misery before.

What if I could just not do either?

"If only it were that easy, kid." A tall, middle-aged woman stood in front of the bed with an oversized white cloak, holding a clipboard as a stethoscope dangled around her neck.

"Excuse me?" I mumbled.

The doctor that had been seeing me ever since I woke up from the coma was a short, elderly man who had a shiny cap rather than a head of hair.

So who was this woman, and where was my doctor?

"You just looked like you were overthinking about something. I apologize if I disturbed you without making a proper introduction. I'm Dr. Murray, and you must be Cadence?" Dr. Murray put aside the clipboard and reached her hand out for me to shake.

Returning the polite gesture, I reached my hand out to hers and gave it a slight shake. As the doctor leaned in closer, I saw her badge read,

"Dr. Mirabel Murray, Physician," with a picture of her to the side of her title. The picture of her was absolutely stunning. She was pictured in front of a white background with slim black glasses that framed her poise blue eyes and subtle pouty lips, and her hair was loosely tucked back with a couple of curly strands of hair left out to distract any flaws that could've been seen (which there weren't any). When she leaned back, I could see the notable features of someone that was well recognizable.

"I'm sorry, but are you by chance related to Mr. Murray, who works at Arkseley High?" I asked.

"Yeah, he's my brother. He has told me a lot about you during the time you were in your coma," Dr. Murray stated as she gave me a demure glare.

"Oh..." I said.

"All good things, trust me." Dr. Murray chuckled with humor.

I laughed along with her, even though I had felt a little bit anxious to know what Mr. Murray had told her about me.

"If life were easy, many of us would be lazy," Dr. Murray suddenly spoke.

She picked up her clipboard that she sat down on the nearest table and started writing down something.

"What?" I said.

Dr. Murray looked up from her clipboard and locked eye contact with me.

"From what I can notice, you are questioning if you should give up or not." Dr. Murray took her clipboard and held it to her chest, peering into what would feel like my soul.

"H-how could you..." I stuttered.

"My brother isn't the only one who minored in psychology." Dr. Murray smirked. "I went through the same things as you have," the doctor began to talk as she made herself comfortable at the foot of the hospital bed.

"Mr. Murray mentioned it to me. But what I can't understand is *how* you were able to move on from it and to be truly happy."

"Well, I can definitely tell you it took time—time that wasn't so generous but allowing," Dr. Murray said as she looked down at her lap and rubbed her hands together with anticipation.

"What do you mean by that?" I asked.

"See, when you go through a trauma like that, it kind of embeds in your mind. That memory or memories will stay with you for a lifetime. Time may allow someone to get past what they had experienced, but time isn't that generous in allowing you to come to terms with what you had gone through. But it's how you go about dealing with your pain—that it is possible that you can dodge less agony that time can render to you." Dr. Murray looked at me again, making eye contact.

"But *how? How* can I be able to come to terms without the pain?" I pleaded.

"You simply can't," she said.

I was sitting up straight and looked at her with more confusion than ever before.

"Pain is inevitable. *Pain* helps us learn and grow from what our experiences have taught us. The best way for you to be able to overcome the pain is for you to simply understand that you have gone through it, you lived it, and now you no longer carry it as if you are still living through it. My dear, sometimes you have to be willing to set aside your anger for the one who has done harm to you to be able to move on," she continued.

My head began to fall, a sign of only distraught.

"So you're telling me that I need to forgive," I said, more of a statement than a question.

"Yes. But do you want to know *how* you'll be able to forgive when you can't forget?" Dr. Murray spoke as if I could hear the positivity ring through her voice.

I raised my head to see her smiling at me.

"To forgive, you need to accept what it is that you cannot go back in the past to change. Focus on your mentality to not easily blame you or anyone else for your feelings and be able to take hold of your own responsibility for how you choose to respond to whatever it may be. Finally, let go of the resentment you may have. When you resent something, you're not allowing yourself to end the situation with compassion, empathy, understanding, or love," Dr. Murray said.

I wasn't crying or even shedding a tear. This was only because I simply knew what I had to do, and I knew how I was going to do it. The confusion that had clouded my sense of reason had now evaporated.

Dr. Murray grabbed her clipboard and made her way to the door, leaving me to my now-renewed thoughts.

Before she could walk out the door, I called out to her, "Thank you, Dr. Murray."

She turned and took a final glance, then she smiled.

"No problem, my dear. Remember this though, you have the ability to forgive but never forget." Dr. Murray gave her last final smile before walking out of the room.

CHAPTER ELEVEN
A New Beginning.

After waiting for Helen to get done with her shift, we made sure that it was okay for me to get discharged. When we got the clear to go, Helen gave me a new change of clothes since the clothes that I had been wearing during the accident were stained with red from the impact of the dashboard.

"Here," she said.

Helen handed me a pair of jeans, a black hoodie, and a pair of socks to change into. When I went into the bathroom to change from the hospital gown to my new clothes, I heard Helen talking faintly to someone. Before I went to the bathroom, I was sure that my mom and I were the only ones in the room.

I put my ear on the cold metal door and listened closely.

"Look, I know that I have to talk to her..." Helen snapped.

As I tried to listen really hard to who the other person could be, I couldn't hear the other person talking.

"I will hang up on you if you won't let me talk!" Helen softly shouted like she didn't want me to hear from the bathroom.

"I know... I'll talk to her on the way... Yes... It'll be done before we see you... Okay... Bye."

Once I had realized that the conversation had been discussed over the phone, I removed my ear from the cold door and wondered who it could've been that she was talking to.

"Cadence, sweetie, are you done changing?" Helen asked from outside the bathroom door.

"Uhm, yeah...almost finished!" I said as I hurried, taking off the gown and changing into the outfit.

Just as I put the hoodie over my head, I noticed in the bathroom mirror that I had a long eerie indent in the middle of my forehead.

I looked in the mirror and took in the full sight of me.

I once saw a girl who hated everything about herself, who criticized her height, her untamable curly hair, and her body's flaws that she had thought were once hideous.

Even though I knew I had some forgiving to do to get rid of the pain that had tortured me, I was seeing this whole other person in the mirror. Someone who I couldn't recognize.

The girl that was staring back in the mirror had amazingly light brown eyes, freckles that were placed evenly among her cheeks, and a beautiful mocha complexion that held no trace of any acne. Despite the new addition that laid on the girl's forehead, she was beautiful.

I was beautiful.

Once Helen and I had came outside the front entrance of the hospital, we made our way to the parking lot that never seemed to be empty.

"Here we are," Helen said.

Helen stopped walking as she went to the driver's door of a black 2018 Chevrolet Traverse.

"Woah, whose car is this?" I asked Helen.

"I thought that it was time for an upgrade. Come, get in!"

Once I got to the passenger side, I opened the door to only be welcomed by the scent of fresh, new leather. As I sat in the passenger seat, I instantly felt uncomfortable as the leather seat was so new that it was like sitting on something that was as hard as a rock.

Helen started the vehicle and began to drive.

"So are you happy that you'll finally be able to come home?" Helen asked.

I wasn't sure whether or not I was happy to go back home. The hospital was a place where I could escape from the everyday surroundings that had influenced the imprisonment of my poisoned misconceptions. To my surprise, it wasn't my surroundings that had infiltrated the obscure thoughts that my mentality suffered.

So really if I were to be honest, I really did miss being home.

"Yeah, I think," I said.

Like you could feel silence's presence, there was a sense of awkwardness that could be detected between Helen and I. It was like we didn't even know what to talk about, if there was even anything to talk about.

When the moments began to feel considerably long, Helen cleared her throat against the stiffness of the air.

"Uhm, I wanted to talk to you about something that I've been wanting to discuss for a while now," Helen said as her main focus was on the road but looked as if her focus was wanting to divert to something else.

With my eyes on her, I replied with an "okay" and waited for her to tell me what was on her mind.

I could tell that something was bothering her.

"Before I tell you, I just want you to know how *hard* it is to talk to you about how I feel. If anything, talking about how I feel to anyone is really difficult for me. See, with how I was raised, I was led to believe that talking about your feelings was a sign of weakness. If you have ever expressed your feelings to someone, then they could just as easily use those feelings—your vulnerability—to their own advantage," Helen explained, as she gave an uncomfortable laugh. "But up till the day you awoke, you had shown a side of you that your *own mother* had never seen. Just then, I realized that expressing your feelings is *not* a sign of weakness. It's something that can relieve any stress or anything that has your mind drowned in confliction. And I think it was only time that we finally had a conversation about everything that you might have a hard time understanding or simply of what I don't understand," Helen continued to talk as she had parked on the side of the main road in front of a bakery.

When the car came to a stop, Helen put the car in park as she unbuckled her seat belt and turned toward me.

"I know that I haven't exactly been the best role model, let alone the best mother, but these past three months have been nothing but an eye-opener for me. If anything, Cadence, I really want to have a better relationship with you. Plus, I really do want to talk about what you have been going through emotionally, as well as what had happened to you."

I unbuckled my seat belt and turned to see that my mom was showing the most adequate sincerity that I could have ever possibly seen before. With my undivided attention, I looked to her in acknowledgment that she was ready to talk about not only our relationship but also what had happened behind everyone's back.

"I know that growing up wasn't the easiest with me being your mother," Helen began to choke on her words but then continued on.

"And I understand if you hate me…bu—"

I raised my hand from my lap and put it on her hands that were in a ball. Her hands were clenched so hard it was as if she had been gripping onto something for so long, they were beginning to turn slightly red.

"I could *never* hate you, Mom," I pleaded.

"Bu-ut the way I had treated you is no excuse, Cadence. When I was little, my mother never showed me affection. So as I grew up to believe by showing no affection or emotion, that it was how I showed my love. I know that while you were growing up, I knew that I might have caused you pain by either body shaming you, putting you down, or simply even pushing you away. And that's not what a parent should be doing to their child." Helen's tears slipped away as if they were trying to hide.

I couldn't help but feel disheartened at the sight of Helen.

My mom was devastated from the weight of guilt that sat on her shoulders, piling up over the three consecutive months.

I was devastated to see my mom hurting from such heartbreak. It pained me to see her crying and to see that she wasn't anything but okay.

"I'm not sure if you can remember what had happened before you got into the car incident, but I said something that I wish I could take back, Cadence." Helen started to rest her head in her hands, removing my hand from hers.

"What did you say?" I asked.

Helen raised her head from her hands, drawing her attention to me. The pain was polished on every feature of her demeanor. Her eyebrows were furrowed in drastic anguish. Her lips pouted in subtle confusion as her deep blue eyes were nothing but a gloss of sadness.

"I said that *I wish I never had you*," Helen sobbed.

The words that Helen spoke were somewhat refreshing to my memory, but yet very sore. Even though I couldn't quite remember my mom saying those words to me, it felt even worse to know that she had said that to me before.

"It's okay," I said reassuringly.

Helen began to shake her head from side to side.

"No, it's not," Helen continued to cry. "You can't even come to your own mother about what you went through, and I wasn't even there to *protect you*. I feel like I have failed you, Cadence. I-I am so sorry."

My mother cried out with every breath that she took.

I looked at her for a brief moment before turning away.

I noticed that she was feeling nothing but guilt and that it had been eating her alive ever since I told her in the hospital.

Helen was brokenhearted, and what was worse was that I didn't know how to comfort her exactly.

"I can't blame you for anything that happened, Mom."

Helen wiped her tears swiftly and looked at me.

"How could you not?" She said.

I couldn't begin to explain how I was tired of assuming that the blame can be put onto Leavan, Helen, or even me. Trying to blame someone to take responsibility for what happened to me was none-theless useless. Before, I thought that there was always someone that should take the blame, let alone for most of the time, I was blaming myself but searched to share the blame with another.

Now I found by trying to accuse myself or anyone else of what happened was futile.

As much as I would love to go back to the past and change things, I can't.

There are always going to be things in the past that we would like to change or correct, but it would be useless to stay fixated on something that we choose to let get to us now.

"I can't blame anyone, Mom. For the longest, I have tried to make sense of how someone else, instead of me, could take the blame. But it doesn't quite work that way. I used to blame myself for everything that did happen—that it was my fault for allowing it to happen to me," I said as tears began to glide down my face.

"No, Cadence." Helen reluctantly placed her hand onto my shoulder in comfort. "It wasn't your fault, and you do not need to blame yourself for *anything* that happened. I want to apologize for everything, Cadence. I know that I have allowed things in the past to happen underneath my nose, but I am so sorry. I don't want you to feel obligated to take my apology—"

"Mom." I looked at Helen with tears overflowing. "I accept your apology. Plus, I don't want you to keep thinking that you need to blame yourself for what happened in the past," I said.

"Hey, look at me," Helen said.

I looked at Helen and noticed that her trail of tears were dry, and her eyes weren't as glossy as before.

"I just want you to know that I had no idea of what your father was doing, let alone what he was capable of. At first, I thought it was really hard to believe because he was the man that *I* had been with. In a million years, *I* would have never thought that your father was capable of doing things like this, Cadence." Helen stared deep into my eyes as I stared into hers.

"I know." I gave Helen a smile to reassure her.

"I love you," Helen said.

Helen had finally been able to open up to me.

She wept her sorrows and told everything that was evading her mind. Helen was able to open up to me.

Above all, Helen and I shared a moment.

This moment was the first of any that had made our bond stronger than it ever was. At this moment, we both smiled and put our heads together—resting our foreheads on one another's. The moment had lasted only for a few seconds until Helen pulled away, but it had felt like we were embracing the moment for an eternity.

"We should probably go inside now," Helen said once she pulled away and rubbed her eyes from any trace of crying.

"Go inside where?" I said.

Helen pointed to the bakery and smiled.

"We are going to pick out a cake to celebrate a new beginning for us." Helen grinned ear to ear.

I never thought that being home would feel any different, but it had.

It felt different knowing that I wasn't going home like any other day to drown in my misery. No, this time, it felt like going home to something new, a new opportunity that awaited me.

"What are we waiting for?" Helen laughed.

The cake was rectangular with white frosting and rose gold lettering with flowers blossoming around the words that read, "*Congrats, Cadence!*"

Helen and I were sitting in the car that sat in the driveway of our house.

"Let's go!" Helen excitedly got out of the car and made her way to the front door—opening the screen door as a cue for me to get out of the car.

Slowly, I got out of the black 2018 Traverse and made my way to Helen. When I got to the door, Helen took the cake out of my hands and gestured for me to open the door. With her hands holding the cake and her back drawing back the screen door, I placed my hand on the sterling silver doorknob. When I opened the front door, I was greeted with balloons, streamers, and confetti welcoming me home.

"Surprise!"

I had seen Lance and Genevieve with party hats on as they were rushing to the door to grasp me within their hold.

"We are so happy that you are home!" Lance said.

I snuggled in between both embraces.

"I am too." I said.

I stood there in their embrace, thinking to myself, it was a start to a new beginning.

CHAPTER TWELVE
A Narrow Road Divided in Two (Part I).

I hated the idea of myself walking around, knowing that my flower was able to escape my own clutches without me even noticing.

Sad to say that while my mom was explaining to me what a flower was and how it can be lost, I had to piece together by myself about what was happening with my own.

The last time I saw him was when I visited him after we had begun our lessons. Even though he had missed my twelfth birthday, he still found a way to send me a card in the mail with a lousy signature scribbled across the bottom. Despite the fact that I felt resentment toward my father, I still loved him. I still wanted to be his little girl who he adored and would do anything for. I still felt the urge to see him, to believe that there was always going to be a way for us to find what was lost—where our relationship between father and daughter didn't feel so odd or even wrong at times.

I still felt the need to care for him, even after finding out what he had been doing to me was wrong for a father and daughter to do.

I didn't know whether to hate myself for letting him do what he did to me or simply hate him for knowing what he was doing.

My judgment was clouded, nonetheless was it in a trance of confusion.

It was as if there were two pathways divided on a narrow road— both being the same yellow brick paths, showing no navigational directions whatsoever. In believing that I was going down the right path in my relationship with my father, I had it pit in my stomach of how unreal this was. It was something that I felt like I had never noticed between a father and daughter, from either watching TV shows or movies or even reading in books. The farther along we had traveled, the deeper my pit grew. Now knowing the actual truth behind the unusual feeling, I regretted taking a walk down the path with my father and not making the decision to prevent us from walking down such a treacherous path.

Knowing the truth of what had been happening scared me.

I was scared that even if I did go back to his house, what would happen?

Not being able to see him for a year has been worrisome since I still cared about him, but at the same time, I had trouble coping with the thought that he didn't have a hard time doing this to his own daughter. My deranged mind had wandered to the possibility of me telling Helen, Lance, or Genevieve.

But how could I?

Not only thinking about the possibility of me telling them of what was happening between Leavan and I was crazy, but also the fear of disbelief and fear of what Leavan would do.

It was like either way, I was at a disadvantage. Telling any of them would just lead back to Leavan, and with the chance of Leavan knowing that I opened my fat mouth about it would probably result in me being in a casket at the young age of twelve.

"Cad." Lance knocked at the door.

"Come in," I announced as Lance swung the door wide open.

Lance was wearing the school colors of blue and gold that was embroidered with a number three on the front and back of his basketball jersey as the wretched smell of body odor invaded the air of which was clean in my room.

"Mom's gonna take you to your dad's. I guess he called her and wanted you to spend the weekend there. She's waiting in the car for you, so hurry and pack your bag," Lance said as he headed to the bathroom— hopefully, to wash the horrendous stench.

It has been a year and a half since I had seen Leavan, and I couldn't make how I felt about staying with him under the circumstance of him calling Helen and demanding that I come stay with him for the weekend. Although I had missed Leavan, I still felt like I didn't want to ever see him again.

To be able to face the man who I mistakenly entrusted was yet too painful to think about.

But what could I do?

I had no choice to pack my overnight bag with my change of clothes and a book that could distract my lonesome mind. Even though I could easily come up with some lame excuse to get me out of going to my father's house, I wouldn't be able to either fake being ill or even keep up with a lie that could probably be seen through by the judgmental eyes of my mother.

As quick as the rushing wind, I grabbed my bag and went out of the front door. When I first walked out the door, the howls of the air brushed against the telephone wires and slightly caressed the left side of my face. I couldn't help but feel a little bit cold since my light-blue jean jacket was very stylish but was not worn to be able to shield anyone from the cold since the jacket had ripples in every seam. Although I was wearing a black turtleneck underneath the jacket and bootcut pants, I still felt a chill crawl up my spine.

I wasn't sure whether or not the stiffness of the cold was coming from being outside or if it was coming from how frightened I was of the idea of going to my father's.

To know the actual truth and still be able to go over there was scary to me.

Again, did I really have the choice?

Even if I didn't agree to go to my father's house, Helen's train of thought would wander to the reasoning behind why I didn't want to go. Then it would lead me to speak of the truth that Leavan desperately wants to keep between just him and I.

Once I got into the car, I noticed how tired Helen seemed as her head was tilted back on the headrest as she wore black sunglasses that hid her tired eyes. With her sterling silver flask on top of the dashboard, she reached forward to grab it, proceeding to bring the poison to her lips.

"Ughh," Helen groaned as she wiped her mouth. "Driving you kids around is nothing but time-consuming," Helen muttered.

When Helen finally put down the flask, she changed gears and proceeded to make her way to Leavan's. Just as Helen was about to turn onto the main road, I started thinking of the narrow road divided into two individual paths.

I stood on the porch of my father's house and waved goodbye to Helen. As Helen backed out of the driveway, she rolled her window down and yelled from across the lawn, "Make sure that you tell your dad that he is going to have to drop you off!"

In an instant, she drove off in a hurry—leaving black traces of what could have been only from her tires.

I turned around and stared at the door that awaited for me to open it.

I looked back down, staring even harder at the doormat that was sprawled out in front of the entrance.

"Welcome home."

The doormat was a dirty brown color that was more than worn out.

It was bathed in mud as the words that were printed on the mat were slowly beginning to fade out of existence.

Now that I was standing in front of my father's house, I was more worried than what I had been anticipating. I could feel my bones tremble in the thought of him violating my well-being. Now that I have been made aware of what he really was doing in our lessons, I wasn't quite sure whether or not I wanted to go inside.

It felt like it was staged as a trap.

No way in, no way out.

"What are you doing out here? Get in the house," my father demanded as he stood there, towering over me like a mountain.

Under his demeanor, I felt little.

I simply felt weak.

In the moment that was short-lived before I went into the house under his orders, I realized that I was a prisoner caged in a cell that I didn't know I was stepping into.

"Go unpack your things in your room once you're done with tidying up the shoes," my father said as he made his way to sit on the brown worn down couch.

Ever since our lessons had begun, my father had started to get a little more strict of how everything in his house looked. He had always wanted everything in the house to be in a certain place, order, or fashion. If something looked like it wasn't in the right spot, he would always ask what it was that was odd about the room. Then I would simply search for any imperfection in the room like I was playing a game of Where's Waldo? Squinting my eyes slightly, I tried to see anything that looked off in the room. When I gave up with defeat, my father would look down at me with an intense stare and point to whatever it was in the room.

The last time I came here, my father got upset that he didn't find my shoes on the boot tray that he kept near the door. Instead, my shoes were to be found by the boot tray lying on the wooden floor. When he had called me into the room, he yelled at me by calling me impetuous for not setting my shoes on the tray like he asked. When I made the exclamation that I didn't want to take up so much space, he backhanded me on the side of my cheek. Just then, he said that he "made this an example" so that I could "never do what I did ever again."

So before I went to go unpack my things that were in my room, I made sure to place my shoes in the boot tray right by his. I made sure that his shoes were straight and neat, as well as mine. I also checked to see if anything else was out of order. When the area of shoes looked tidy, I went to my room with everything that I had brought and started to unpack my belongings in the room.

My room at my father's house was nothing big nor small. It was a boxed room with white walls and a white bed.

The room was nothing but dull that screamed captivity. Since I didn't live with my father, he thought that it wasn't necessary to have the room without a closet or anything that seemed permanent. So he got me a white mini dresser with five drawers to put any of my clothes/belongings in.

Already settled in, I walked to the living room to see my father already downing a bottle of whiskey he held firmly in his dominant hand as he sat on the brown worn down couch with his eyes glued to the TV.

When he noticed that I was watching him, he waved me over.

Moving my feet to where he was, I stopped in front of his view.

As he patted the seat to the left of him, I took my place by his side. Trying my best to scooch closest to the arm of the couch, he wrapped his arm around my shoulder and pulled his body to sit entirely too close to me.

"Now, did you miss your old man?" He smirked and brushed his lips against my ear.

With each word he spoke, I could smell the whiskey that laid in his breath.

I turned my head away from him.

I was disgusted.

"Hey, you better look at me," my father said as he aggressively grasped onto my face, making me turn to look him square in the eyes.

"Hey," he began. "Did you hear what I said?"

Although I cared deeply about Leavan and had missed him, I wasn't going to admit it. I wasn't going to cave into the idea that I did miss him, for it would only boost his ego.

Shaking his grasp off my jawline, he retreated his hand back as he sighed loudly in my ear.

"It's fine. I don't need you to admit what I already know," my father said as he placed his hand that was closest to me on my lap. "I already know that you missed me," he said as his hand crept toward my inner thigh.

Before I knew about my flower, I would have thought that every part of this scene was nothing but normal. I would have told myself that it was okay for his hand to be there, for his fingers to lie where they were. I would have felt as if this was a way for a father and daughter to bond.

Before knowing about my flower, I would have thought that it was okay for him to be doing this.

But now, I didn't know what to think anymore.

Although I wanted to stop it, I couldn't.

I was his prisoner, and I didn't know what I could do to escape. If anything, I thought that I wasn't ever going to be able to escape, even if I could.

Like he could feel how uncomfortable I was becoming, he removed his hand and caressed the side of my arm before getting up off the couch. With his whiskey in his hand and the remote in the other, he turned off the TV and retreated to his bedroom.

"Be in my room in ten minutes. If not—" my father turned to face me before entering his room—"I will come get you myself." My father disappeared after walking past the threshold into his room of darkness.

I couldn't help but weep.

I was stuck and left again with thinking of the narrow road divided into two paths. Not knowing whether I could or couldn't break free of my imprisonment to the path I was already on.

CHAPTER THIRTEEN
A Narrow Road Divided in Two (Part II).

I couldn't sleep.

I was lying in the stone-cold sheets that brought no warmth to my body. Even though I began to shift in the lonesome sheets, nothing had brought my body any sort of comfort.

I could feel the restlessness that had found my company quite entertaining, and I couldn't bring myself to lie silently. Like it was a reflex of mine, I quickly sat up in the bed and banged my head against the bars of the headboard. As the back of my head exploded from the outburst of pain, the headboard rang with clarity as the white cast iron couldn't help but share the excitement from clashing with my head. When I felt the pain throb under the felt tips of my fingers, it seemed like the pain couldn't help but burrow its way deeper into my brain—causing the normality of my train of thought to become a bit dazed.

I easily rolled my neck in a circular motion in hopes of exempting the pain from continuing anymore, but instead of alleviating, the pain quickened its race. With blood rushing to my head, I started to feel the intense pounding that would only bring a migraine.

Even though I knew I didn't bring any medicine for headaches with me, I came to the realization that I would have to go ask my father if he had anything that would help.

But I didn't want to.

Although I dearly wanted to be rid of this migraine, I was scared to ask something that would seem of little importance to wake him up in the dead of night. It felt silly to ponder about how he would react to me waking him up, but at the same time, I didn't want to lie awake with this arousing migraine.

With the movement of my hand, I took hold onto the white sheets and swung them over to the other side. As I got out of the bed, my feet slowly started to walk in front of the other, making their way out of my room and to my father's bedroom door that was to the right of mine.

As I opened the door, I could easily hear the creak the door exerted that made its presence known in my discretion. With the light that was radiating in the hallway, it had bounced off into the room—clearing any ways of darkness with its profound illumination.

With the first step past the threshold, the floorboards had started to squeak beneath my feet. Besides the loose floorboards, I quietly made my way to my father's bed and stood before him.

My father was lying on his back as he drew in deep, steady breaths.

I felt like a statue who was posed in an awkward stance that was towering over someone.

At the sudden creaking of the floorboards underneath my feet, my father shifted his body on his side to face me. Still with his eyes closed, his breathing became more rapid.

I tapped on his shoulder that was closest to me. As I waited for him to open his eyes and become aware that I was in his room, he did nothing but remain in the same state.

Instead of tapping on his shoulder, I let my hand easily take hold and gave it a stern shake.

Once again, he didn't wake up.

My father was still breathing, as his nostrils flared when he inhaled.

For him to not wake up at the sudden shake of his shoulder was astounding.

With nothing coming to mind of how I was to wake him up, I suddenly called out for him aloud.

"Dad!"

Like waking up to a siren, he jumped up in fright and looked around his room until finally meeting my gaze.

With anger written in his expression, he glared at me with frustration for disturbing his deep sleep.

"What the fuck, Cadence!" My father yelled as he threw his hands up in the air and then slammed them back down on the surface of his sheets.

It was as if a pin dropped.

With the window to his room opened, you could only be able to hear the outside noises that clashed with the sound waves of the room. The wind rolled off the tree branches as the leaves clapped with full excitement. The moon had sat high in the sky as little spectacles surrounded it—showing that the moon wasn't the only thing that could fulfill the night with iridescent light.

"What the hell do you want?" Rubbing his eyes with the palms of his hands, he was trying to wake up from what could've easily been a dream.

"I-I was-s just wondering if you had any medicine for a m-migraine?" I questioned as I let my hands grasp one another behind my back nervously.

My father sighed in exhaustion as if I were something that he wished he wouldn't have to bother with.

In a sudden rush, he moved his sheets and swung his legs over his bed for them to meet with the creaky floorboards. With a sour look, my father looked at me and then got up to walk out of the bedroom.

As if I was in a hot pursuit, I followed after my father, who was striding toward the kitchen. With each step he took, the whole house shook from the quake of the stomping that his feet had made.

Making his way to one of the cupboards above the microwave, he opened it to reveal a series of rows of medication. Some of the medications were prescribed, whereas the others were over the counter.

"Take this," my father demanded in a stern voice as he handed me a white tablet with a bottle of water.

I placed the tablet on my tongue as I twisted the cap off the water bottle. When the cap was off, I drank the water as if it was pure gold. Swishing the water down, I felt the pill slip down my esophagus as it made its journey to my stomach.

"Now come to my room." My father turned his heel and proceeded to his room.

I didn't want to go into the bedroom, for I already knew what was about to happen. Let alone, I didn't want it to happen... not ever again. With me already knowing what he was doing, I let him fully take advantage of me yesterday. And yet, I had done nothing to prevent it from happening.

He took advantage, and I couldn't manage.

I couldn't manage to speak up and stand up for myself when I knew that it was wrong.

Was I wrong to not stand up for myself?

How could I?

I couldn't do anything but squander in fear at the thought of not obeying him at the time when I knew that it was wrong.

I let him take advantage of me yesterday, but not now—not ever again.

So I decided to stay in the kitchen.

A couple of minutes went by before my father popped his head around the corner.

"Didn't I fucking tell you to meet me in the room?" He asked.

My father came out from the corner of the wall to expose that he had no shirt on, as well as wearing nothing but clingy black boxers.

Trying my best not to look directly at my father, I looked around the kitchen. Noticing there wasn't really much to look at since the kitchen held nothing but the appliances, I couldn't help but divert my sight to my father, who seemed to take a couple of steps closer to me than before.

"I said—" my father made two long lunges toward me, gaining more of my personal space—"didn't I tell you to come in the room?" He grumbled, gritting his teeth.

Looking up to my father, I could tell that my disobedience had agitated him even more.

Beyond scared, I tried to come up with an excuse as to why I wasn't comfortable going into the room with him. But then it was as if every word that I planned on saying to him wouldn't come out, as if the words were stuck and didn't want to be said aloud. With every ounce of courage that I could muster, I only was able to say the few words that would enable me to get the point across.

"N-no, I don-n't want to," I muttered.

Silence couldn't have been any more quiet than what it already was.

My father moved in closer, gazing down at me with such intensity I felt as if I was going to explode like dynamite.

In a quick swift movement, my father's right hand met my neck—taking hold of the circumference of my neck. I couldn't help but feel as though I was trying to hold my head above water, gasping for some sort of air.

"You think I was asking?" My father laughed as he found that choking me was fulfilling his amusement.

I tried placing both of my hands onto his wrist to try to pull his grip off of my neck, but his strength overpowered my will.

I tried to the best of my ability to push him off of me, whether by kicking or hitting his arm, but found that I was having a difficult time trying to pry him off of me.

"Listen to me, and you listen carefully," my father said as his right hand came to grasp my neck tighter, and he pointed his left index finger at my face. "Don't think that you have an option. Do you want to know why?" My father said, not really interested in whether I wanted to know or not. "You are an object to me. You only have one job in a man's life, and that is to please him. Nothing more, nothing less. You're not allowed to have a say in whether you want to do something or not. Believe me when I say that you will never amount up to anything significant in a man's life besides bringing him pleasure. You're worthless, Cadence. Face it. Whether it be me first or another, you'll be used in many ways. I'm just preparing you for the remainder of your miserable life." My father smiled in satisfaction.

Was it possible that I was beginning to hate myself?

Was it wrong for me to believe that everything he was saying was true?

The cruelty of his words was convincing enough. They felt like knives stabbing me in the back. But even with every word that he said to me, I wouldn't have ever thought that this is what he thought of me.

This was what he had thought of his own daughter.

It was hard for me to comprehend that he was capable of thinking this way of me when I was six, and we drew butterflies together, when we had spent quality time together—before hell broke loose, and he looked to me as someone other than his daughter.

I was brokenhearted.

Where did the man I grew to love go? And who was the stranger that was taking advantage of me? Who was this man who was casting all these pitiful comments onto his only child?

Above all, why did I feel as though I was guilty of opening the door to someone who was disguised as my father?

"From now on…you won't ever defy me," he said.

As if he was carrying me as a butcher was to carry a chicken by its elongated neck, my father threw me on the arm of the brown, worn down couch. With the arm of the couch uncomfortably lying among my stomach, my father let go of my neck and took the initiative of covering my mouth.

I was past the point of trying to stand up for myself.

I knew defeat when I seen it.

With my tears no longer able to hold themselves collectively, they slid down my face with familiarity.

Just as I thought things couldn't have gotten any worse, my father bent down and lightly spoke in my ear.

"Don't think that you have an option," my father whispered before standing up.

The night ended with him finishing and taking a cold shower.

As for me, the night ended with me crying in the corner of my room with nothing but no hope.

I wasn't able to believe that the narrow road was divided into two paths anymore. If anything, the narrow road held the path that I was already on, and this path that I was on led to nothing but doom.

CHAPTER FOURTEEN
The Sticky Note.

I couldn't believe that everything that I had experienced within such a short time frame led me to want to turn a new leaf.

Turning a new leaf by which is to only let go of the resentment and hatred that I had against my father and be able to move forward by forgiving him for doing the uttermost damage to my past self.

Trust me, not for one second that passed by I thought to myself that it was going to be easy—because I knew it wasn't going to be.

It was like walking on a treadmill.

I was so used to speeding my way in one spot but never had realized it for myself, let alone did I figure that it was leading me to walk such a configuring trail that would only lead me to my down-fall. It was as if I was only trained to be on the treadmill, thinking that it was my only option.

Little did I come to find that there was a solid ground that I had a choice with walking upon. Only that the catch would be that I had to let go of the very things that I thought had bound me to the treadmill.

Not only was it the Murray's and my reality that persuaded me to want to walk a different trail, but also including my very own decision.

If seeking any improvement from prior states of your life, the most alternating choice to change is only going to come from what you choose to make of it. Although you jump from the treadmill to the solid ground, you still have to put in the effort for yourself to make the change, which can be hard—but not unattainable.

Before putting my feet on the solid ground, I feared that I wouldn't be able to attain a life without the pain lingering. But fear not, if truly coming to the terms of your change of heart, nothing can linger from your past life—this including the pain that has followed you wherever you may have gone.

But as I paid attention to what was going on around me, this including the signs of coming to terms with touching the solid ground, Mr. Murray lecturing me on forgiveness, my reality, Ms. Murray on how she dealt with her superstitions, Helen opening up to me by expressing her pain, this I knew that I could lead a life without the unbearable pain I grew to come to comfort with.

Although I was comfortable with walking in the same spot, reaching no final destination, I had the sense that I would finally be able to gain a different type of comfort that would give me rest on the solid ground—that of which those who lead me to make the decision to get off the treadmill had done.

Even though it had taken relentless time to discover the solid ground and make my way to taking a step onto it, I finally did it. Although I couldn't have done it without those who made me realize that there is more to life than staying in the same destructive spot, I owe myself a lot of much credit for being able to take a step on the solid ground and making the decision to follow a different path that was meant for me.

Knowing that with taking a step on the solid ground, I knew that I had to take a journey down the path of recovering from what harm has done in the past—making myself renewed in the image that pain has not inflicted within me but yet has been turned into light from darkness. This being able to call myself a survivor from the tormented mentality that has caused me such heartache by being conflicted with the pain that had stored itself in the premises of my entire being.

It's not going to be easy, but with each step that I take on the solid ground, it will be worth being free from the troubles that held onto me as I stayed on the treadmill that never went anywhere but to my ruin.

The solid ground is not meant to be easy but attainable. If anything, it's meant to be challenging for you to become something better than what you were before.

It was my first day back to school since the car incident, and I couldn't help but feel like I had never walked within the hallways of Arkseley High. The hallways had been glorified with Arkseley's famous blue and gold colors that were to be seen dangling from the ceiling, as the mascot of a hornet was plastered on posters with a cap and gown painted on them.

But as usual, the students still paraded through the hallways as if they hadn't seen the new decor that made the hallways full of excitement. Although the students paid no mind to their surroundings, the familiar faces I had once taken acknowledgment of before the car incident was now looking at me as if I was a mystery.

All of a sudden, those familiar faces that were once looking at me started to talk quietly among others. Circling in clusters, they would look at me and then look back to those who were around them.

Standing in front of the office of Arskeley High, I moved quickly to somewhere others wouldn't care to look.

Despite my utter confusion as to why everyone had their eyes on me, I came across the janitor's closet that was isolated in a little hallway. Being back at school, I couldn't help but feel as if everyone had been watching my every move, like I was an exotic animal at an exhibit. Never before had anyone paid attention to what I was doing, nor did they care either.

It felt extremely odd to me how every student was looking at me like they either knew of me or wanted to.

I pulled my phone out of my blue jean pocket and sent a message to Genevieve.

Where are you?
Cadence

At your locker. Where are you?
Genevieve

In a janitor's closet.
Cadence

What the…why are you in a janitor's closet, Cadence?
Genevieve

I'll fill you in at the locker. Be there in five.
Cadence

Tucking my phone back in my pocket, I looked around in the janitor's closet to see dust collecting on the wooden shelves. Everything in the janitor's closet looked as if it hadn't been touched in eons.

With the twist of the doorknob, I opened the door to hear a loud ring clash over the announcement speakers that could be found all throughout the high school. As if it were a rush hour, students were bolting out of the classrooms to get to another class.

Like there was actual traffic, the right side of the hallway headed to the east side of the building, whereas the left side took you to the west side of the building. Without drawing any attention to me, I swung into the student body that traveled to the east side of the building—leading me to my one and only locker.

As the students trampled over one another to reach their destination, I removed myself from the herd of students when I could see my locker in the distance.

Genevieve was leaning her shoulder up against my locker with her phone in her hand. When Genevieve noticed me, she waved me over as she gave me her flashing smile that had everyone glaring.

"Hey!" I said when I finally reached the locker.

"Why were you in a janitor's closet?" Genevieve questioned as she couldn't help but chuckle.

"Everyone has been staring at me, literally. Some people were even looking at me while talking to groups, *and* they were whispering. What did I miss?" I said with confusion.

Genevieve's smile was no longer being worn so fondly as it once was. Instead, her lips pursed together into a straight line.

"Well…" Genevieve began but then stopped for a minute before continuing. "While you were in your coma, the school board took recognition of you and made an announcement of your absence. A lot of the students and staff had thought you weren't going to make it, so I think it's only a shock that they saw you today. I don't think anyone knew that you woke up," Genevieve stated as she pushed herself off my locker and sighed.

I couldn't be upset at the thought that others didn't think I was going to be able to wake up from the coma. Although I was genuinely moved that the school board had thought to acknowledge the tragedy to the students and staff, I didn't think that it was worth all the staring and sideway glances everyone was giving me. Never had I gotten this attention before, and neither had I wanted it.

"Look, right now, it's lunch. If you don't want to go to the lunchroom, we can go wait in the bathrooms or even sit by your locker," Genevieve said.

Genevieve was beyond a good friend. If anything, she was someone who I saw as a sister. She stood collectively with her long curly hair held tight in a bun and her brown eyes gleaming down at me. She smiled. I couldn't help but share the smile that I found very contagious from her.

"Mhmm…although both suggestions sound pretty rad, how about we just sit in the lunchroom?" I said amusingly.

I couldn't settle with the thought that my best friend was willing to give up a seat at the lunch table just to ease my discomfort.

Despite the crazed looks that rendered my way in the lunchroom, I couldn't care less. The underlying feeling that they were seeing someone who woke from a coma felt different. Although the staring was nothing but sympathetic, I saw it as if they were witnessing the wake of a totally new person.

This person to others could have easily been seen as mysterious or glowing with such radiance, but if anything, this person felt different to the eyes who have walked the hallways of Arkseley High because she had been mentally and emotionally reborn.

And this person was dying to make her presence fully known to not only Arkseley High but also to everyone who came across her path.

At the last ring of the bell for the school day, I sat in my usual seat by the window in Mr. Murray's class, taking in the view once more.

My breath was stolen as it had been before looking at the view.

"Everyone, let's give a warm welcome back to Cadence Palmer." Mr. Murray clapped his hands together in delight as the class applauded right after.

Again, the students continued to stare but then gave their attention back to the teacher.

"Cadence was in a coma for merely three months, and although some had their superstitions that she wouldn't be able to see her next sunrise, she had proved them wrong," Mr. Murray said aloud, drawing even the inanimate objects' attention back to him. "Which brings us to our next prompt," he said as he began to take the white chalk to the chalkboard.

In his perfect cursive, the board had read, *"How do you have the ability to change others' perspective of what is possible for your future."*

Once Mr. Murray had finished writing, he took a step back from his chalkboard and stood to the side.

As he waited for a student to raise their hand, I looked around the room to notice that no one was talking or even on their phone. Nevertheless, all the students in the classroom showed no signs of being distracted, rather than they were more attentive to knowing what Mr. Murray's prompt implied.

As no one had raised their hand, Mr. Murray looked at me.

"The prompt isn't rhetorical. Therefore, there is only one reasonable solution to what the prompt is saying." Mr. Murray took his eyes off of me and looked back at the chalkboard. "You can't."

With everyone taken back, I could hear the slight dramatic gasps coming from the back rows. Mr. Murray had never written a prompt that wasn't rhetorical. He had always thought that there was always more than one way of seeking a solution from his prompts.

"No one is going to be able to decide your future, but *you*. Whether you are unsure of what the possible options are in store for your future or not, no one is going to be able to change the minds around you but *you*. If you choose to lead a life that has been built on a destructive foundation, you're going to lead those around you to believe that you have a possible future with nothing good to offer. But whatever you may choose in your future, it's your narrative. By saying that it is your narrative, I'm also saying that it shouldn't matter whether or not what others think of where you're going or how long it will take you to get there—but it does matter that you know that whatever you may choose, it is *your* narrative. So don't change your narrative to prove your point to someone else that something, in particular, is possible for your future, but know that *you* have to prove that particular something is lined up for your narrative," Mr. Murray said.

The classroom went silent before the crickets really started buzzing throughout the room. Before someone could raise their hand to go to the bathroom to escape the harsh silence in the air, Mr. Murray spoke again, "With that being said—" Mr. Murray picked up a crisp white envelope that sat on his desk, waiting for him to open it up.

"Seniors, when I call you up, please come get your tickets for the graduation ceremony."

The ceremony tickets were for those who we choose to invite to watch us walk across the stage when each graduate gets their diploma.

But as if I were stuck in another era, I had no idea of how close we must've been to be receiving the tickets for our friends and family to attend the graduation ceremony. Then again, I wasn't in school for three months, and it was already May. In less than three weeks, I would be walking with my classmates across the stage to get my diploma.

To ensure that I was going to graduate on time, the school board recognized me as being in a coma as excusable. This was because the second semester for seniors was only busywork.

By the time Mr. Murray had called out every senior, he picked up the last remaining tickets as he called out my name.

"Cadence," he said.

In a fast motion, I got up from my seat and made my way to Mr. Murray.

"Here you go," Mr. Murray said.

The three tickets were pastel yellow that had the location of the ceremony, which was our gym, and then it read, "*Pass.*" Making my way back to my seat, I couldn't help but think of who I wanted to be at my graduation ceremony.

Despite not really being close with any family member besides Helen and Lance, I had one other ticket to spare.

My thoughts couldn't help but avert to giving the ticket to my father.

The last time I saw him, he was very urgent on getting me home as quickly as possible. My father and I hadn't either spoken or seen each other since, but not that I wanted to anyway. I'd figure that it was the best way for me to keep my distance without being asked what happened between us.

Although I knew that it wasn't necessary to invite him, I felt that it would give me a chance to take a step in the right direction in becoming something other than holding a grudge against someone who I not only needed but also wanted to forgive.

As the last bell rang, the students got to their feet and hit the ground, running to the door. I was still sitting at my desk as everyone else was leaving, finishing up what I was writing on the plain sticky note that I took out of the front pouch of my backpack.

Rushing to catch up with Mr. Murray, who was already out of the classroom, I swung my backpack onto my shoulder and held the sticky note that was stuck to a ticket.

"Mr. Murray!" I shouted from down the hall.

As the hallway was cluttered with bodies, I saw Mr. Murray make his way out of the doors before I shouted his name.

Like an obstacle course, I maneuvered my way through the hallway to Mr. Murray with what I had possessed in my hand.

"Could you be able to mail this for me? I don't think that my mom would allow me to, even if I did ask," I said.

Mr. Murray looked down at what I was gesturing to him to take, looking at me as if he had to ask who I was sending it to. And as if he understood who I was sending it to, he gave me a slight frown.

"Are you sure?" He asked.

"Please," I said as I reached my hand out to him that held the ticket and sticky note.

Mr. Murray then gave me a nod and took it.

CHAPTER FIFTEEN
Graduation.

I looked in the mirror and couldn't help but not take my eyes off what I had been seeing.

In the mirror, I had seen a girl wearing a white lace dress that traveled just below her knees and branched off her collar bones in an elegant way, making her appearance look beyond flattering than what she could've expected from a cheap thrift store.

Just slightly covering the upper half of her dress was her navy blue gown that was longer than her white dress but still flowed off her dress to where people could see that the gown wasn't clingy to her frame. But the most eye-catching thing that the girl in the mirror had was the navy blue cap that sat on top of her head. The cap held a tuft of threads that hung loosely of blue and gold. At the top of the tuft of threads, the number twenty could be seen.

The girl in the mirror was beautiful.

I was beautiful.

"I'm glad we were able to get your cap and gown on time," Helen said as she brushed past my door to stand by me.

As Helen came to my side, she tucked my hair behind my ear and began to rub my shoulders in comfort.

"Beyond gorgeous. You know, I am really proud of you, my love," Helen said as her eyes met mine in the mirror.

I smiled at her, and under her gaze, I felt such an immense love radiating from her presence.

It had been a couple of weeks that I attended school after the car incident, and lucky for me, those couple of weeks had been the last remaining days for the seniors to be present at Arkseley before graduation.

I couldn't begin to comprehend that today was the day that I was going to receive my diploma—nevertheless, was it the day I couldn't be less prepared for.

Before coming to the realization that I wanted to embark on the journey for my healing process, my senior year had to be the most challenging for me. Prior to senior year, I never gave a thought to what life would be like for me outside of high school. Most of all, I wouldn't think that the life I wanted for me would ever happen. The life where I would be happy and be able to experience new things without feeling as if there were a void I had been desperately trying to fill.

Senior year hit me hard because I had no clue what I was going to do, especially *who* was going to be there for me when I had decided what I was going to do. Never did I fail at comparing myself to other people and their lives and who was exactly taking part.

I felt as if I was a loner standing in a crowded room.

When I looked at myself and compared it to another's, all I could see was that they had reliable parents in their lives—a mother who could work a nine to five while still engaging in her kids' life and a father who would've never given a thought to abandon his children.

Having my eyes wide open, I envied what others had.

Little did I know that the envy would pick up the feelings that I embedded for quite some time, all to make the feelings come up to the surface.

But again, that was at the beginning of senior year.

Now being at the very end of my senior year, I have come so far.

There was a point when I was consumed with no hope for being able to attain happiness, when thoughts would roll from the back of my mind, whispering the most dreadful things one couldn't imagine about not being able to walk among those who have found their happiness in their times of darkness.

I wouldn't have ever thought it would be possible.

But it *is possible.*

I have no doubt that it is a process to overcome, but the process is worth it. I know that it will be worth it because having this glimmer of being free from the shackles that controlled me for so long has been relieving enough already.

"Thank you," I uttered as I blushed.

Helen leaned her chin onto my left shoulder and gave me a hug from behind.

"We should get going. You have to be at the elementary school in twenty." Helen laughed as she swiped away a few tear droplets.

Every year, Arkseley High's graduates go to every school in the district to walk the halls of which we attended before we reach the high school for our ceremony—call it a stroll down memory lane before reaching the present.

As my mom took my hand to pull me from the mirror, I gave myself one last look. Although I didn't know what laid ahead for today, or even tomorrow, I knew that I needed to take one step at a time.

So here goes one step toward the door.

Just when Helen dropped me off at the elementary school for the walk, I saw a bundle of people who were wearing the same cap and gown in front of the entrance. Guessing that is where we were supposed to gather before taking the walk through the elementary school, I walked over there only to be interrupted by someone jumping onto me.

"Hey-y! Are you ready?" Once I gained my balance back, I noticed it was Genevieve who scared the daylight out of me.

Genevieve was beyond stunning as she wore a simple white dress that was in the form of a "V" at the hemline and floated slightly above her knees. Besides wearing her white dress, she wore her navy cap and gown just as the rest of us.

"Woah...you look fantastic, Cadence!" Genevieve claimed excitedly.

"Look at you! You're beyond beautiful, Gen." I smiled.

As if the moment couldn't wait to last a little longer, a man who was dressed in a black-and-white tuxedo stood up in front of the mass crowd of seniors and cleared his throat.

"Seniors, listen up! We are going to begin to walk through this building, then we will take the bus to our middle school, and then you guys will be heading back to the high school for your ceremony. Now who's ready to take *the walk*?" The man yelled.

In spite of every senior knowing what the outcome was after the ceremony, they were more than ready to take the trip down memory lane as everyone began to jump up and down while screaming at the top of their lungs with joy.

"While you guys walk, you *will* be good examples for the young ones. So that means no foul language while you're walking, *and* you will walk in an organized line of two. So, everyone, choose *one* partner to walk beside you. With this partner, you're going to sit next to them on the bus as well," the man in the tuxedo said for all to hear.

Just when I was about to turn to Genevieve to ask if she wanted to be my partner, she entwined my arm into hers and rushed to take a place in the front of the line.

Once we had taken our spot up front, she looked at me.

"I can't begin to tell you that I am glad I am doing this with you. I wouldn't want to do it with anyone else." Genevieve smiled.

"Me too," I said.

Once we had stepped inside the entrance of the building, it was as if my five senses were activated, and every memory felt as if it had come into perspective.

There were little red and blue cubbies outside of the classroom doors that held each students' backpacks or belongings, as there were paintings on the concrete walls of animated characters doing little activities of either singing, dancing, or learning something. As we walked down the corridor of classrooms, the teachers began to release their students to come out of the classroom to applaud us.

As the little kids clapped their hands and waved "hi" and "bye" to us, there were times like this where you're in the moment of being celebrated for your accomplishments. Whether they knew it or not, it felt like they knew of how hard I had been struggling to find my way out of the shadows, how tough it is to lift yourself when others can't.

It just felt like a victory worth celebrating in disguise.

Once all the seniors had paraded throughout the entire building, we departed as a group to go greet the teachers we once had and came to adore. When everyone was done visiting with each other, every senior began to head back to the bus to get ready to go to the middle school. Once Genevieve and I were seated, I could hear someone close sniffle as if they were trying to be discrete with their crying. As soon as I turned to face Genevieve, she was looking down while quietly trying to mask what was upsetting her.

"I can't believe how far we've come, Cad. At this point, I really don't want to graduate. I don't want to grow up," Genevieve cried.

In response to seeing my best friend crying, I slid my hand onto hers and held onto it.

"We're growing up together." I smiled. "And that's what matters."

Once we had reached the middle school, we did the same as we did at the elementary school. The only difference was that the middle schoolers were more frantic about our visit and seemed to not really care for our little celebration.

Now we were at the high school, and it was just moments before the seniors would be allowed in the gymnasium to be seated.

As I waited to be seated in the gym, my anticipation was beginning to get the best of me. With no patience left, I peered through the doors to see hundreds of people sitting among the stands who were talking with one another or even getting their cameras ready.

No doubt, every senior was catching nervous breakdowns. It was like everyone was beginning to become hysterical at the thought that they would trip over their feet and fall.

"All right, everyone, line up for roll call!" The man in the tuxedo yelled.

Just as we were shown in rehearsals, every senior scrambled to form a line and got out the white cards that had their full names printed on the front of them with how the speaker should pronounce it correctly.

Once the man in the tuxedo made sure that the formation of the senior student body was assembled in an adequate way, as well as making sure that everyone was accounted for, he made the signal for all of us to begin to walk through the doors into the gym.

Just when the gym could be heard from miles away, the noise began to dim quickly as people caught sight of the navy caps and gowns. When the seniors could be seen walking through the doors of the gym, everyone turned to look or either move their cameras onto us to record. Regardless of being a part of the ceremony or not, you could always hear that one person—or more—shouting their graduate's name, followed by a "*Woohoo.*"

When we finally got to our seats and began to settle down, the lights started to become dimmer and dimmer. The only light that could be seen was the few spotlights that were trained on the broad stage with chairs that were lined up to the left with a podium standing on the front part of the stage. As the seniors were seated, the school board members began to walk across the stage to be seated in the chairs that stood proudly on the stage. Each school board member was wearing a black gown and cap with a V-like sash of different colors across their collarbone that carried itself past their shoulders and onto their backs.

In my perspective, they all looked like magnificent scholars of the highest degree. If anything, they even walked the part that they were dressed as. Immediately, after the school board members took their place in their seats, one member who was very tall and had black stern glasses made his way to the podium and began to speak into the microphone.

"Welcome friends and family to our seventy-first annual graduation ceremony! My name is Mr. Worthwal, the superintendent of Arkseley Community Schools, and on the school board's and graduate's behalf, we would like to thank each and every one of you for coming out here to celebrate the finest class that our establishment has ever seen…class of twenty-twenty!" Mr. Worthwal announced.

As the ceremony had continued to proceed with more speakers to visit the podium, my mind and sight were distracted elsewhere.

Although I wanted to just jump out of my seat and find my father, who was I to actually think that Mr. Murray would've done as I wished?

I mean, any other teacher wouldn't have gone out of their way to deliver a silly little ticket that could mean less to them. But even though the thought of Mr. Murray throwing away what I gave to him could be surreal, it didn't strike me that he would be that thoughtless to not help out a student who was trying to do her best to resolve current matters.

The more that the ceremony was continuing to go on, the more I felt the need to panic.

Would he *really* not want to see his daughter graduate?

If Mr. Murray had mailed my father the ceremony ticket, then it would be a good chance that he would be here.

So why was I worrying?

"Cadence!"

I turned my head to my left at the sudden whisper of my name coming from a fellow peer of mine who was in Mr. Murray's class with me.

"You have to move. It's our row's turn to walk on the stage!"

Being the first one to the right of the row would mean that I would have to walk on the stage first, following behind the last person of the previous row.

At the sudden rush for me to fasten my pace to the stage, I kept in mind to walk gracefully but manage to speed walk to make it on time.

Just as I had seen the last person from the previous row make it to the other end of the stage with his diploma, I instantaneously gave the speaker who was announcing the names my white card. Then I went to the steps to get on stage and began to walk toward the superintendent to get my diploma.

Just as if Michael Jackson couldn't say it any better, I literally felt like someone was watching me. In my case, *everyone* in the gym was watching me walk across the stage. As if I was a model, I pretended to walk down a runway as I avoided any eye contact whatsoever with anyone.

Just as I reached the superintendent, he gave me a shake of his hand and turned me to the audience for those who wanted to take pictures of the graduates. Even though I tried my hardest to see through the blinding lights, I still wasn't able to see my father. In a matter of half a second, the superintendent smiled and then handed me my diploma.

While I had the diploma in my hands, I started to make way toward the other end of the stage. From the stage back to my seat, I was left with nothing but hope that my father would show up tonight.

The night began to come to an end as the superintendent congratulated every senior then had us take our tassel and move it to the right side of our cap. When everyone in the gym cheered and clapped in our accomplishment of finishing high school, the seniors took their exit to go find their families and take pictures with one another. It was truly a sight.

Through tight spaces, I found my mom and Lance talking to Mr. Murray, who could be seen standing near the doors of the gym. As I started to close the gap between them and me, I noticed that Lance was carrying a bouquet of the most exquisite white roses.

"Hey!" I said as I rushed to Lance, embracing him in the tightest hug.

"Hey, Cad!" Lance smiled.

As I pulled away from Lance, I could tell that something was bothering Mr. Murray. Although he was smiling fondly, he was twirling his fingers in a manner where someone thought he couldn't focus on anything else. I knew all too well that this was something very unusual for him to do.

"What's wrong, Mr. Murray?" I asked.

Before turning his head to look at my mom, who shared the same expression, he let out a long sigh.

I wasn't sure whether or not to freak out because I didn't know what the matter could be, but I wasn't going to be led into thinking that it had nothing to do with my father's absence.

In a short instant, Mr. Murray pulled out a crumpled envelope from deep within his pocket and handed it to me.

Unopened, I began to tear through the envelope to reveal what I couldn't have ever thought it would conceal—the ticket.

"I mailed him the ticket to the address you gave me, and this was mailed back to me," Mr. Murray claimed.

Taking the envelope out of his hand, I stared at it, noticing that it was crumpled, had sloppy handwriting, and reeked of tobacco.

My heart couldn't feel anything but sorrow.

I felt as if I couldn't sink any lower than this.

Did he not love me anymore?

Was I not good enough?

Despite my want to recover from the damage I endured, it felt like another plunge of a dagger in my heart.

"I believe you," I said to Mr. Murray.

"I don't know if this will change anything, but you don't need to have a relationship with your father to move on. You have enough love present with you right now. Who needs your father when you had a brother who basically took care of you as his own, even when I couldn't?" Helen spoke out of the silence as she looked to Lance.

"Cad, I know you feel like you need to have your father to admit that he was wrong for putting you through what he did to ease your guilt or the blame you have on yourself, but, Cad, you need to forgive yourself. You shouldn't seek out his guilt to relieve your own.

Find it within yourself," Lance said as he gave me the bouquet of white roses.

"Most importantly, your father was a part of your life for a reason, and that is to teach you something that you will be able to carry throughout your life. Sometimes, the things that we try to hold onto aren't worth holding onto. Sometimes, things are hard to let go of, but why hold onto something that had already let go of you?" Mr. Murray said.

Although it pained me to hear the things that were coming from not only my family but also Mr. Murray, I knew that they were right.

I looked at each one of them and saw that I wasn't on this journey alone. I had my brother, who was always there for me whenever I needed him. I had my mom, who changed her ways just to build a relationship with me. I had the wisdom that had been passed down to me from the most stupendous teacher a student could ask for. And even though Genevieve wasn't exactly with me at the moment, I had her to always count on.

Sad to say that even though I was seeking out for my father through it all, I didn't take the time to appreciate what was standing in front of me all this time.

"What did I miss?" Genevieve shouted as she was overjoyed and wrapped her arm around my shoulder.

As we all began to laugh at her sudden but hilarious outburst, somehow we entwined in a group hug.

Although I planned on seeing my father for the first time in years, I knew that I didn't have to. Although I planned on receiving some sort of apology from my father, I didn't need it. Although I planned on telling him what he put me through, I didn't want to.

Though I am still traveling down the path that I need in order to heal, it's a process.

But the final end result is worth the process.

Sometimes, closure arrives in a way you never expected.

But it will come, and when it comes, you'll be completely free.

I am a warrior whose wounds are no longer bound by the flesh and unforeseen to the eye; but a warrior whose no longer scared to assist to the lesion's wounding that yields pain.

—Casslynn P.

ABOUT THE AUTHOR

Born and raised in Flint, Michigan, Casslynn had started writing at the age of nine and grew up to graduate at Kearsley High School on the honor roll. Despite her accomplishments of enrolling in speech contests and writing her first book, she is an advocate for those who have no voice to speak out against sexual and mental abuse. She aspires to be not only a good author but also a motivational speaker, willing to help those who are in need.

CPSIA information can be obtained
at www.ICGtesting.com
Printed in the USA
BVHW042220271021
620160BV00006B/112